INTO THE
AETHER

To/ Jo & Matt

*Hope you enjoy my book!
Thanks for the support.*

*Natalie
Xx*

NATALIE RIX

INTO THE AETHER
NATALIE RIX

Published by Monnath Books

Monnath Books

Copyright © Natalie Rix 2018

Cover design and book formatting by James Waltho

All rights reserved.

ISBN: 0993134815
ISBN-13: 978-0993134814

DEDICATION

Thank you to my wonderful parents and friends for supporting me with my writing and my dreams of becoming a published author. A huge thank you to James for always helping and supporting me and aiding me with the creation of this book. And to Michael Talbot, one of my favourite authors, who loved to delve into the concepts of mysticism and the interconnected nature of the universe. Without reading The Holographic Universe and his fiction novels, and his sheer open-minded enthusiasm for trying to explain the unknown, I probably would never have been inspired to create this book.

CONTENTS

ENTER THE DREAMSTATE 1

MY PODGE 17

FILE CORRUPTED 39

THE HAZE 60

THE PHOENIXIS 93

THE OVERWRITE 118

THE PRINCE'S TAVERN 141

GYPERIA 2138 164

THE CONDUIT 184

ODESSYA'S RAGE 204

According to ancient and medieval science, **aether** (Greek: αἰθήρ aithēr), also spelled **æther** or **ether**, also called **quintessence**, is the material that fills the region of the universe above the terrestrial sphere. The concept of aether was used in several theories to explain several natural phenomena, such as the travelling of light and gravity. In the late 19th century, physicists postulated that aether permeated all throughout space. Hindu philosophy states that Akasha or aether is the fifth physical substance, which is the substratum of the quality of sound. It is the *One*, *Eternal*, and *All Pervading* physical substance, which is imperceptible.

ENTER THE DREAMSTATE

A moment ago, Erik had been in his local coffee shop, The Daily Grind, but now he was somewhere else entirely. There had been no transition of movement. He thought it was a rather sarcastic but apt name for a coffee shop for it was always full of people running businesses from their laptops and chugging away at endless cups of hot caffeine. He was one of them. It was his regular which he frequented nearly every night to try to catch up on his mass amounts of paperwork for work the next day.

Erik had worked in the administration side of a local architectural company for the last twelve years. His new boss was really laying the work on him lately, expecting him to do the work of three people, and he'd been finding it difficult to cope.

The daily grind indeed, he thought. And now he was where? He wasn't sure.

The atmosphere was different, cool, like being submersed in a cold pool but without the flow of water around him. Far different to the warm interior of the coffee shop. The air had a thick blue tinge. It looked magical and ethereal.

He floundered for a moment as he tried to gain some composure of where he was. He felt as if he should be panicking, but the gloopy, dense air made him feel so calm he could barely even rouse the emotion within him. It's not like he had the energy to panic anyway.

Maybe I'm dreaming.

But it didn't feel like a dream.

Maybe I'm dead.

It was the next logical conclusion. He couldn't remember dying or even falling asleep. He squinted, trying to peer through the undulating waves of blue. A brick wall became visible through the less dense waves. He was sure that he recognised the area, but it looked much different to usual. The atmosphere was deceptive, betraying the features of a place he was sure he knew.

If only he could think of it.

Instinctively, he attempted to walk forwards to investigate, but instead he just floated.

Woah!

He looked down to see that his feet were a few yards higher than the floor.

I'm floating! But how?

He held his hands out before his face, blinking rapidly as he tried to focus on them. He then wiggled his fingers, as if that would somehow discern his solidity. But the atmosphere was dense and his vision kept wavering. He struggled to keep lucid against it. It felt like a deep lethargy he was powerless against. He couldn't really feel his body.

Maybe it is a dream. A very vivid dream...

A faint muffled noise in the distance which sounded almost like traffic caught his attention.

He propelled his body forwards through the air by sheer will, examining the brick wall. It was covered in graffiti. The blue tinge in the air was lessening now as the brightly coloured tags of spray paint on the wall became more visible.

Looks like the back of Café Dream Bean, he thought. The Daily Grind's rival. A building he'd done contracting work on just last year.

What is it with the weird coffee shop names?

He floated past a dumpster overflowing with rubbish from the city. The noise of the traffic became almost audible as cars whizzed past, clocking around 60 mph, yet they seemed to inch by so slowly that he could see the wheels spinning gradually.

The city... he thought, realising he was passing through some locked gates towards a busy main road. There was no sensation of the metal bars as he passed through them. The road heaved with night time traffic.

Dim balls of light floating at different heights in the air suddenly caught his attention. Erik turned his head to peer at them. Their shapes changed, shifting in the air before him. It looked like they were changing into slightly luminous shapes of people, but he couldn't quite tell.

He floated backwards as he stared right at the lights, trying to fathom them, not realising he was heading straight for the stream of oncoming traffic. As soon as he realised, he tried to scream, but didn't have time to react. His body fell down in slow motion right as the car ploughed into him, through him. He waited for the pain of impact, but it didn't come. His eyes were wide with astonishment as the structure of the car entangled with his flesh and spirit, momentarily layered together.

The woman driving the car yawned, glancing at the illuminated digits on the digital panel next to her steering wheel. It read 23:57. She shivered as Erik floated through her. She glanced at the window, looking for a breeze, but it was locked. She shrugged, and then the car passed through him and onwards down the road.

Erik shook himself out of his reverie and floated out of the road, astonished as to how he had remained unscathed from what should have been a fatal incident. If he was what? Awake? Alive?

He struggled to turn his body around in the gloopy atmosphere, like paddling against a current. He turned to the dim lights that had distracted him and made him fall into the road. They had been dimmed due to the thick gloopy atmosphere, but now they were all shining brightly, revealing a large number of ghostly people floating around eerily.

Maybe I am dead.

A man floated past him, a bit higher up in the air. He was a middle-aged, lanky Jamaican man wearing faded blue jeans and a shabby brown coat with a sweatshirt underneath. His face looked vacant and expressionless. His long greying dreadlocks rippled behind his head as he moved.

"Marcel?" Erik said, suddenly finding his voice. The sound of it shocked him as it echoed around him. It didn't sound like his own voice. At least it was audible, unlike the muted sounds of the traffic.

He wasn't sure how he knew the man's name. He felt quite certain he had never seen him before, yet somehow he seemed all too familiar.

Marcel turned towards Erik, his expression pinched as if annoyed, but his face suddenly lit up when he recognised him, as if he had also been shaken from his dreamy reverie.

"Erik! My friend. Didn't your mother ever teach you not to play in traffic?"

Erik managed to smile. Marcel had a glow about him that made Erik feel calm, happy and safe. The positivity radiated from him. He seemed like some sort of spirit guide. Erik suddenly felt warmer.

"Who are you? Where am I? How did I get here?" Erik asked as he floated alongside Marcel. They wafted down the main road together.

Marcel shook his head slowly and strenuously, as if trying to combat the friction of movement against the dense air. The pinched expression returned.

"Not again. You never remember! We literally have this conversation every time we see each other," he replied, somewhat disgruntled. His hands were clasped behind his back as he swished forwards.

"I've been here before?" Erik blinked slowly. His voice was still slow and distorted, as if the sound waves struggled through the dense air.

Marcel nodded.

"Where is *here*?" he furrowed his brow, puzzled, determined for answers.

Marcel sighed. "You are in your city. Do you not recognise it?"

"I thought it looked familiar, just doesn't seem right. I feel like I'm dreaming."

"That's because you are dreaming. We're in *The Dreamstate* — an astral plane that houses a collective consciousness of people who travel here when they are asleep. This realm is different to our normal internal dreams because we are all lucid. Our consciousness is external to our bodies. This astral plane, like all others, run parallel to each other. They are all interconnected, easily accessible for non-material beings to slip through."

Erik floated on silently, feeling nonplussed. He was still certain that this was nothing more than a ridiculous dream. It had to be.

There was a long silence between them as the pair both mused on what Marcel had just explained.

"Thank god I'm not dead," Erik finally said, using humour to cover his fear and wonder of this bizarre experience. His voice sounded slightly more animated now.

Marcel smirked. "I wish you could remember our astral encounters so that I don't have to keep explaining. I said hello to you the other evening in waking life, with the hope that you would remember me, but you just looked at me like I was mistaken."

Erik frowned as he remembered. Marcel was a homeless man that had started sitting outside the coffee shop a few months ago. He sometimes absent-mindedly threw some spare change into his hat as he rushed back to work. "Ah, um, that was you sitting outside the coffee shop on Tuesday night?"

Marcel nodded.

"Oh, I'm sorry," Erik said.

"It's fine. It's understandable. This is a different level of consciousness."

"How long have I been coming here?"

"A couple of months. We met the first time you came here and we've become good friends ever since. I've become your spirit guide, so to speak."

Erik smiled. "I got that vibe from you." Erik reckoned he could do with a friend at the moment, what with all the chaos in his waking life.

"You work too often, too late at night. Propping yourself up with coffee and energy drinks and having no decent meals won't do your health any good. I can sense your energy draining dramatically. If you don't change your life soon, you will burn yourself out. You need to rest. You need to concentrate on your creativity, on your interest in photography. I have to tell you this now because it would be difficult to tell a stranger in waking life."

"But I have work to do. I can't let go of my pay check for a hobby that will probably never even take off. It's too much of a risk. I have some huge

7

deadlines coming up at work. I just don't have the time to rest." Erik shook his weighty head. His energy seemed to dull upon talking about work, diminishing in luminosity, turning dull grey.

"That's why you're here. It's your soul's way of escaping mundane life for a while. Sleep is a retreat for the mind and the body."

Erik turned to notice where they were floating, watching the awake people going about their daily business, completely oblivious to their astral presence.

"Dartmouth Avenue," Erik read aloud the words on the metal street signpost. He swam forwards. The atmosphere now felt thinner, lighter, or perhaps he was just getting used to the sensation now. "I know this street. The coffee shop is around the corner. My, erm, body should be there."

"Flaked out over a cup of coffee and a work assignment, no doubt," Marcel tutted, but his tone was caring.

As they floated around a corner, they were suddenly hit by an overwhelming feeling of darkness. They felt it before they saw it.

"We need to be careful," Marcel said, his brow furrowed.

Erik squinted. He could see a dark shade of black hovering in the distance, a black hole of energy, a vortex deeper and darker than the night. It didn't appear to have a corporeal form like their astral selves. It was magnetic, drawing them closer. Erik looked down to see particles of energy being drawn away from his body, darkening from a luminous blue to black as they were engulfed by the hidden damaging influence. Erik felt like the presence felt familiar which disconcerted him. Was this dark entity someone he knew? Was this person's true form hiding behind a throbbing mass of darkness?

Erik struggled, trying to float away in an effort to repel the dark energy. It was tiring, trying to conserve every particle of his diminishing energy, almost like trying to swim against a strong current.

Marcel positioned himself protectively in front of Erik. His body rippled with pulsating lights, deflecting the negative energy away from them. There was a high-pitched screaming whisper and the darkness retracted into the nearest building.

"How did you do that?" Erik gasped, trying to catch his breath and regain some energy as he was left floundering in the air, feeling even weaker than before.

"Humans are beings of energy. We need energy to survive, through sleep, nutrition and emotions. Our consciousness resides within matter in the physical world, physical vessels such as our bodies. We are all full of positive, neutral and dark energy in varying degrees. But it is our choice to decide what energy we let into our lives, and what force of energy we project — a positive or negative energy."

Erik wrinkled his nose. "That's true, but sometimes people don't realise they're being negative or they've been tainted by toxic relationships or environments. It doesn't necessarily make them a bad person. They just don't know any better until someone casts a light on them." Erik cast his mind back to the toxic effects his vile ex-girlfriend had had on him. He hoped he was a better person now he had cut her out of his life.

"That's true," Marcel mused. "But I'm not talking about poor misguided souls. There are extremely dark energies out there, energies that know they are sinister and don't care, those that enjoy it even and actively thrive on it, but I don't want to burden you with all that tonight."

"Like that thing we just experienced?" Erik stared off into the darkness, feeling horrified.

"Yes. A malevolent energy which leeches from and consumes from others. The world is full of them, influencing the awake people from beyond the astral veil, but they can too be overcome by benevolent energies like us. We choose to muster our own energy instead of steal it from others."

"That energy seems so familiar," Erik shuddered.

Marcel's eyes widened. "Then be careful. It may be someone you know personally."

Erik had some ideas, people he hated, but he couldn't be sure. This energy was far darker than even the most horrible people he knew, unless it was their interior darkness manifesting itself in all of its menacing glory. They floated towards The Daily Grind.

Marcel saw a dark wisp leave the building and

float across the road. "Its energy has been greatly diminished. It's retreating. Let's follow it."

"Do we have to?" Erik cringed, not wanting to be around the energy at all.

"Come on. Don't be frightened."

They cautiously followed the dark shadow at a parallel distance, watching it filter through another wall of a building. Erik recognised the place but he still peered up at the sign above the window. The Daily Grind.

"Uh, oh," Erik muttered.

They followed it through the wall to see it hovering near a young woman sitting in a corner stall. Her hair was set in a small tousled bun, her neck decorated with strings of multi-coloured wooden beads. Early twenties, dressed in a formal two-piece skirt suit. She stared desolately into the pages of a book she was obviously not reading, her mind elsewhere.

"I've seen her before. Poor woman always looks miserable," Erik remarked. He was becoming increasingly worried watching the dark presence float up to her, swirling around her ominously. It terrified him that the awake people couldn't see it, that the woman couldn't see it. He shivered, wondering what invisible entities might lurk around them every single day.

The woman seemed to sense it, though, like a sixth sense. She suddenly stared in its direction, peering around as if someone was watching her.

Erik noticed the other energies floating around the coffee shop, popping in and out of existence, to and from other astral planes. How bizarre that a freeway of energy portholes existed all around them within the aether, invisible to the human perspective.

Some of them were different colours and hues. Now he vaguely understood what chakras meant, different layers of spiritual energy. His colleague Amanda always talked about chakras and crystals. He thought she talked a load of rubbish. But now, it was obvious that these energies all had varying, tangible, real-world effects on the people they were hanging around. Some were influencing their loved ones, some were floating around aimlessly, appearing lost as they travelled through this astral plane, some seemed oblivious to the alternate level of consciousness, simply returning back to their human bodies when they awoke. Erik wondered how many of these energies were actual ghosts, the ones that never return to their bodies. Perhaps there was no distinction.

The dark energy began to absorb some positive energy from the young woman. It began to float away from her in huge iridescent swirls. The sudden change of mood was instantly visible in her expression. Her lower lip started to wobble and her eyes became watery. She suddenly started to cry, throwing the book down onto the table. She covered her face with her hands, pushing her mobile phone across the table.

"I knew I wouldn't get the job. I'm useless! I'm never going to get a job," she sobbed quietly, trying to hide her face so nobody would see her anguish. The happiness drained from her face as the presence began to suck even more energy from her. She was descending rapidly into melancholy.

"Hey! Leave her alone!" Erik found his voice, shouting loudly. He felt so angry, watching that thing literally suck the energy out of the young woman.

Erik floated upwards in the air, propelled by the urge to come to her aid. He wanted to do something to help. He flew up to the dark shadow, a glowing ephemeral bluish white light and knocked it away from her. He felt a stark pain from the impact, from the sudden clashing of raw energies and the mixing of forces. Some of the black swirled in the air and was engulfed by Erik's power, black turning luminous blue this time. The shadow recoiled, letting out an unnerving scream of anguish, a deep hollow rasp that sent a chill through the air.

For a split second the outline of a body was visible within the swirling black mass, like it had been illuminated by a flash of lightning. There was an evil cackle within it.

"Next time you won't be so powerful. I'll be waiting..." a deep, inhuman voice reverberated from within it. It retreated, flying away out of the building.

The woman stopped crying, peering up from her hands. She wiped her tear-stained cheeks with the end of her sleeve and reached over to her phone. She smiled weakly, like the mood had passed and she was feeling sheepish for crying in public.

"Sorry to hear that your interview didn't go well. Their loss. You're a hard worker and a great person. You'll find something soon, don't worry." Her smile became wider as she read aloud a consoling text from a supportive friend. "How sweet."

Erik turned to see Marcel floating by the bar, looking shaken by the attack. "You're more powerful than you think, buddy. Just that one action made a positive impact on someone's life."

Erik felt pleased. He wasn't one to mess in other people's business, and he'd never really cared enough to go out of his way to help strangers, but now he felt a thrill from his altruistic act.

They watched the woman shove her book, notepad and mobile phone into her Boho-style handbag, then get up to leave. Her metal bangles rattled as she pulled her handbag onto her shoulder.

"Hey, I should be here some..." Erik felt like he was falling, like in a dream, like his energy was being pulled elsewhere. He woke up suddenly with a start, his body jumping in his seat. "Where," he mumbled, peering around him. The bright glare from the artificial lights stung his eyes and the pungent smell of stale coffee made him feel sick.

"Hey, sleepyhead! Nice of you to rejoin the land of the living! You were well gone," his colleague and friend, Amanda, smirked as he sat up properly. He stretched his arms out, trying to recall the events of his dream.

"Was I asleep?" he yawned croakily, rubbing his

bleary eyes. He ruffled his mousy blond hair with his fingers. He grabbed his coffee cup, swirling the cold dregs around the base, taking a swig to combat his dry mouth. He immediately regretted it. The taste of the cold coffee made him retch. "Yuck!" he spat it back out into his cup.

"Yup, for about half an hour. I used that time to check the contracts. We still have to go over the details of the building supplies. They need to be in tomorrow at ten," she yawned, thrusting some papers towards him.

"We've already been over these contracts a million times. They're fine," Erik groaned, staring blankly at the papers. His mind was elsewhere. Remnants of his dream were flooding back into his mind. He remembered Marcel, and the woman, and that thing.

What a crazy dream.

A bell swung on the main doorway. Erik looked up from the papers to see a woman leaving the shop, handbag slung over her shoulder: the woman from his dream. She walked past the window with a smile on her face, a look of renewed hope in her expression.

Could it have been real?

Erik remembered his conversation with his spirit guide, Marcel. He remembered everything this time. It had been real.

A wide smile spread across his face. "You know what, Amanda?" he said, getting up and putting his jacket on.

"What?" she asked bemusedly, hastily collecting the papers back up.

"I'm going to bed."

MY PODGE

It broke my heart to watch them in bed together, kissing, cuddling and laughing. Talk about moving on quickly. I had only been dead for a couple of months and he was already dating another woman. It seemed like he had moved on so quickly. They couldn't see me as I stood watching at the end of the bed. They were oblivious to my presence. It hurt so much that this woman, Andrea, was enjoying his comfort the way I used to. He used to be mine. He was my everything.

I was glad that they couldn't see the tears falling down my cheeks or hear the dry sobs that I could not contain within me. All I needed was some chains to rattle and I would be sorted, full-on ghosty.

I had seen how upset Podge had been at my funeral, how he had broken down when they had lowered my coffin into the furnace, how he had been torn with grief when he helped my parents scatter my ashes across the lake we used to camp near every summer holiday.

I'd seen everything.

My Podge.

His real name was Max but this was the nickname I had given to him when he'd got a little bit podgy last Christmas. It was funny how his fitness fanatic football buddies would rile him for it. I had affectionately joked that it was more to hang onto. He had lost all that extra weight now, from the stress and agony of my sudden death. He hadn't even been back to play a game since.

My untimely death had arrived so unexpectedly. That damn stupid driver shouldn't have crashed his lorry straight into my little blue Peugeot. I hadn't stood a chance. Aged twenty-three and at the start of my nursing career, engaged, and planning to get married, I had my whole life ahead of me. My life had been drastically cut short, and there was nothing I could do about it but stand here and watch, watch Andrea take everything I had. She was a pretty little thing, the perfect sort of woman, with long blonde hair down to her pert ass, a cute little button nose, and a twinkling smile.

God, I hated her.

I envied the way she ran her hands over his now slim body and cooed at him like a besotted little schoolgirl with a crush. What does she know about him? She wasn't there for him during the hard times like I was. Doing it in our house, too — in our bed! Did the last three and a half years of our relationship mean nothing to him?

I got angry, wanting to smash something. Perhaps I could become a poltergeist and freak them out, like in all those horror films we used to watch together — a detached spirit wreaking vengeance from beyond the grave on those who had wronged them.

Andrea turned her elegant head and saw a cut-out paper love heart with our photo on it, pinned onto a cork board on the far wall of the bedroom. "Did Sophie make that?" she asked.

Max nodded, solemnly.

But then I saw his reaction and changed my mind about haunting them. I saw the emotional flicker in his eyes when he gazed into hers, almost choking down the fact he couldn't look into mine anymore. He faltered, looking down.

"I'm so sorry. I shouldn't have asked." She held his hand supportively in her own.

"It's okay. It's only been a couple of months, you know. I am trying to act normally. Well, as best as I can." Grief overtook him and he bit his wobbling lip. He pushed his legs out of the bed and sat on the edge, looking downcast. Andrea sat behind him, pressing her svelte body against his, hugging his back, her head on his shoulder.

My heart fell as I saw him. I wanted to reach out to comfort him. I would do anything to get the chance to be able to touch him again, to hold him and lovingly stroke his hair. I walked around the bed and stroked his hand.

Sensing something, he suddenly looked up, staring right at me. I froze, thinking for a moment that he had seen me, but he just looked around and shrugged off the paranoia.

"It just makes me so angry that she was taken

from me like that. I feel so vulnerable that one minute you can have everything, you think you're safe, planning life and plodding on like you're sure things will remain the same forever. Then you wake up one day and your whole life is altered forever. I feel stupid for thinking it would never apply to me."

Andrea remained silent, not sure what to say for the best.

Sensing how the tone had become awkward, he turned to face her, taking her in his arms to reassure her. "Look, it's nothing against you. You know how I feel about you. I love you. I just need to take things slowly at the moment."

The words "I love you" made me pang with grief.

"Of course," she nodded, a glum expression falling over her pretty face. They both sat there looking solemn, uncomfortable in the silence.

I felt gobsmacked. Perhaps I'd been too judgemental. I was upset and had let my emotions get the better of me. I knew I shouldn't be angry with him. I didn't want him to be alone, not really. Had I somehow expected him to mourn and wear black for the rest of his life, to throw himself under a bus with the vagaries of grief in an effort to be reunited with me? No, that was horrible, and I had been selfish to even think he wouldn't miss me. Perhaps Andrea will be good for him. I just wished it was still me instead of her.

I watched them get dressed, kiss each other goodbye, then I watched her leave and Podge sit there for hours, staring at the love heart. I was surprised he'd kept that silly little token. It seemed such a pathetic and irrelevant indication of my life, but memories were all that was left of me now.

No, that wasn't true. I was still here.

He opened a little jewellery box and took out his engagement ring. He rotated it between his fingers, smiling wistfully as he read aloud the inscription on the inside of the ring.

"*To my Podge*... Funny how she loved to call me that daft nickname," he smiled between tears, slipping the engagement ring onto his finger. He seemed to gain comfort from hanging onto it. I wanted to cry. This wasn't consoling at all, it was agonising.

"I am still here, Podge," I cried too, and crept onto the bed next to him. I put my arms around him, whispering words of comfort that remained unheard.

After some time, he finally fell asleep.

I watched him sleep for a while, feeling like a spooky voyeur, feeling creeped out myself. What ghosts had looked over me and invisibly guided me when I had been alive?

I am a ghost, a spirit, a corporeal essence with no bodily limitations. It was that moment an awful thought struck me.

No, I couldn't... It was a despicable idea. I scolded myself for even considering it. I wanted to possess Andrea's body. *Despicable, but brilliant.*

Wondering if the idea would work, I went over to Andrea's house. I just *had* to feel Podge again, to tell

21

him everything that I wanted to, no matter how much that would scare him. Perhaps I needed to do this to pass on, or whatever the hell that was going to happen next.

Perception was different in the afterlife. I still had the image of my body, but it was just a spectral form spirits hang onto to cling onto the life they once had. But as I discovered, it was possible to dispel my form and turn into a conscious spirit on the wind. It was fantastic to join the elements, become one with nature, within the aether that all matter and consciousness permeated. This is how I travelled. I could sense where Andrea was. I envisioned her, and I was there.

I materialised in her kitchen. She was perched against the kitchen table, manicured hand wrapped around a steaming hot mug of tea. I walked around her, getting a whiff of her poncey herbal tea. Camomile, I think. Another woman was sitting facing her. Middle-aged and plump. Sallow skin sagged under her baggy eyes. She looked like she hadn't had a good night's sleep in some time.

"Is dad feeling any better today?"

"He managed to sit up earlier, but he couldn't eat anything again. It's not looking good, I'm afraid. Doctor Emil is coming to talk to us tomorrow about his condition."

There was a solemn silence as they both stared disdainfully into their mugs.

"I'm sorry I didn't go to visit him today," Andrea said. The tone of her voice was soft, vulnerable.

"We'll go tomorrow." Her mother patted her hand affectionately. "How is Max?" she asked in an effort to change the subject. Her voice was gravelly. She coughed, resting her lighter upon her packet of cigarettes.

"Oh, mum. I don't know what to do for the best. I'm trying to be supportive of him and his bereavement, but it's hard to deal with."

I rolled my eyes. *Sorry to be such a nuisance in your love story.*

"What with everything that's going on here, I want to tell him about my problems, but I don't think it's fair. He's had enough grief without lumping mine on to him too."

"Give him time, love," her mother coughed again, glancing at the packet of cigarettes and wondering whether to light up again or not. "But he should be a sympathetic ear to you as much as you are to him."

"Yeah, I suppose. We've only been dating a couple of months, though. I just hope I'm not rebound."

"If anyone thinks my girl is rebound then they've got another thing coming," she chuckled, placing an arm around Andrea's shoulders.

"Thanks, mum."

"Things will blow over, love. Just you see. It just takes time," she nodded. She picked up the packet of cigarettes that had been tempting her and headed for the back door.

"Thanks. It's been a long day. I'm knackered.

Think I will go to bed. Night, mum."

"Goodnight, love."

Andrea kissed her mother on the forehead, and then headed upstairs to bed.

I followed her up the stairs, one dainty step after another. Andrea turned around on the landing, looking around, but not seeing me. Her shoulders slumped down as she retreated into her bedroom.

"Urgh!" I gasped as I entered her overly girly bedroom. Pink bed throw, light pink wallpaper with a pink floral overlay, and pretty sparkly things here and there. Vomit-inducingly pretty. There were framed photos of her with family members. I saw a large photo of her cuddling up to an older man, probably her father, plus many photos with friends from various raves, wearing neon body paint and glow sticks for bangles. She wasn't the sort of woman my Podge would go for. Feeling disgruntled, I pushed a glittering vase from the shelf and it landed with a crash on the carpeted floor below.

Startled, Andrea stood frozen to the spot, clutching the edge of the desk of drawers next to her bed.

"What the hell?" she muttered as she teetered over to the vase. She picked it up gently, closely examining the shelf as if to determine the cause of its fall.

"Argh, it's broke. I'm going to have to find some glue now," she sighed, placing the pieces of the cracked vase back onto the shelf.

I floated behind her as she walked towards her wardrobe. Loosening her long hair from a high ponytail, she opened the wardrobe door and peered into the inside mirror.

A faint grey face appeared in the mirror, my face reflecting from behind her.

She gasped, turning on the spot. The colour drained from her tanned face as she gaped open-mouthed. The terror was visible in her eyes as they widened dramatically, her mouth contorted with fear as she was unable to scream, unable to move.

"S-Sophie?" she managed to stammer.

I smirked, the right side of my mouth lifting, my gaze looking more psychotic than I intended it to. Trembling like a frightened rabbit, she attempted to bolt for the door, but tripped over the side of the bed. She crashed downwards, quickly swivelling so she was sitting upright, hugging her grazed knee.

"What do you want?" she cried.

"I want my Podge back!" I snarled. My voice sounded hollow and sinister, even to me.

"Who?"

"MAX! I want him back. I want back everything that you stole from me, everything I hold dear!"

"No," she sobbed. "I didn't steal him. He's mine now!"

That did it.

I flitted closer, vanishing and reappearing inch by inch. Terrified, she screamed, and in an effort to get away from me, stood up and ran towards the door.

Feeling furious, I flew straight at her, falling rapidly into her body. She staggered forwards, clawing at her temple, grunting as she struggled with me inhabiting her. It was the most peculiar sensation as my spirit invaded her flesh. I felt like a parasite taking over, two sentiences vying for the same space, constantly rebutting one another in an effort to take control.

Get out of me! I heard her scream. Possibly inside my head, or was it outside? I couldn't be sure. I didn't care.

The body moved towards the mirror. I tried to stop it, but Andrea compelled it forwards. Hands gripping the edge of the frame, knuckles white, we saw our face. I could see my own visage beyond hers, a scary mesh of my own features mixed with hers.

Get out of my fucking head! I could hear her, feel her, sense her thinking. She was a fighter, but I was more powerful.

I felt dizzy as I felt her kicking around, a constant surge that was trying to regain dominance. The constant internal yelling made my head spin.

Shut up, bitch! I yelled back at her, inside of her own head. The image of my bloodied, dead face had now settled back to her gentle coquettish features. I smirked, satisfied that I was now in control and headed towards the door.

It was ironic and hypocritical that the body I hated Podge touching, the body that turned him on, now seemed pleasant to inhabit. It felt good to be in a body again, even if it wasn't mine. The assimilation and harmony of body and mind is something I always took for granted when I was alive. All of the bodily sensations were a thrill to feel once again, to feel the physical components of emotions: heart racing, stomach tied up in knots, knee throbbing with pain. I could feel all of her woes and worries, how desperately depressed she felt about her terminally ill father.

It was a shame, but it wasn't my problem.

I raced down the stairs and grabbed Andrea's car keys from a side table.

"Hey, are you okay? I thought I could hear banging upstairs," a gravelly voice came from the shadows. Her mother was laid out on the sofa watching television, staring at the screen like a zombie, her mind obviously elsewhere, no doubt mulling over her husband's impending death.

"I'm fine. It was nothing," I replied coldly.

Mum, please help me!

I narrowed my eyes as I opened the front door.

"You sure? You seem different," her mother said, hobbling over towards me, pulling me into a hug. I grimaced at her touch because it might bring Andrea forth, annoyed because I needed to leave.

"I'm fine. Don't worry." I tried to smile reassuringly, patting her on the back. She stared at me, eyebrows raised, definitely sure that something was up. Mother's instinct, I supposed.

"Okay, then," she conceded. "Where are you off

to? I thought you were tired."

"I'm just going to see Podge," I replied, gritting my teeth, taking another step towards the door.

"Who's Podge?"

"I mean Max," I said hesitantly, putting half my body through the doorway. I had nearly slipped up.

"Oh, okay. Don't forget, we have to be up early in the morning to go to the hospital."

"I know. I won't be long. Be back soon."

"See you, love."

I headed through the door.

The cool breeze felt so refreshing. I closed my eyes and enjoyed the fragrant night air. I threw myself into the car and turned the keys in the ignition. My fingers began to pull away from the steering wheel, possessed by Andrea. With some difficulty due to her resistance, I managed to push my hands back onto the wheel. I gripped it tighter. I pulled the mirror down and glared at myself, at Andrea specifically, warning her not to mess with me. Her sobs rattled around my head, or her head, as I pulled the car away and drove to Podge's house.

I felt giddy with excitement as I pressed the buzzer on Podge's front door. He used to go crazy when I'd forget my keys after my night shifts at the hospital and had to wake him using the buzzer. I heard footsteps crashing down the stairs. Podge opened the door. The hallway light dazzled me as it shone out into the dark street.

I had been watching him since I had died, but this

was different, knowing that I could feel his touch again, his warmth, his love. Sudden nerves overtook me. My throat was dry and sweat beaded my forehead. He looked so handsome as he ruffled his messy brown hair, yawning. A strong hand propped him up against the doorframe as he peered out sleepily at me. I noticed he was still wearing the engagement ring. Perhaps he did miss me after all.

You leave him alone, you psycho!

"Andrea? What's up? It's nearly one in the morning." He yawned again.

Max. Max! It's not me...

I crashed into him, wrapping my arms around his waist, breathing in the enticing smell of his aftershave, and holding him like I never wanted to let go.

"Hey!" He smiled affectionately, looking down into my eyes, stroking my new soft blonde hair. "What's brought this on?"

My eyes filled with tears. "I just needed to see you. You have no idea how much I've missed you."

"After an hour? Okay then, come in," he laughed and ushered me indoors.

We headed straight to the bedroom. We sat on the bed and I held his hands in mind. I had missed this so much.

Max!

Without hesitation, I pushed my lips onto his and kissed him passionately, tasting his sweet lips and running my fingers through his hair. Andrea was furious. I flinched as she rammed me internally. A pain shot through my head, making me wince. I couldn't stop crying. It was overwhelming to be back in his arms.

"Whatever has gotten into you?" he asked worriedly, putting me at arm's length to survey me, a hand clasped onto each shoulder, gazing directly into my eyes.

"M-M-Max!" a voice stammered from out of my mouth. Andrea had finally managed to speak.

"Yeah?"

"Oh, Podge, I've missed you so much!" There were so many things I wanted to say, so many things I wanted to tell him, but I felt speechless just looking at him.

An expression of confused bewilderment fell over his face, his eyes searching mine suspiciously. He frowned. "What did you just call me?"

"My Hodge Podge." I broke down.

"How did you know to call me that?"

"Because that's the nickname we gave you when you put on some weight and got podgy last Christmas. It was more to hang onto," I sobbed.

"I never told you that story." He let go of my shoulders and started shaking his head, seeing my true face flicker over Andrea's. The colour drained from his face and he looked aghast.

"No. No. It can't be!" He started to back away.

I grabbed his arm and pulled him back closer.

"Sophie?" His eyes simmered with the emotional turmoil that was bubbling within him.

"Yeah, it's me!"

"How?"

Tell her to get out of me!

"Wh-where's Andrea? You've possessed her?"

"She still in here. She's fine. Dormant. I went to her and explained my plight. She agreed to help me speak to you again," I lied.

You lying bitch!

A weak smile overtook his startled confusion, and he gingerly pulled me closer into an embrace. His body was rigid with fear. "My Sophie, you came back to me. I've been devastated."

"I know how much you've been hurting. I've been watching over you constantly." I gently stroked his cheek with a thumb.

"Constantly?" He thought about all of the times he had been intimate with Andrea and felt sick that Sophie had been watching.

"I love you so much, Podge. You are the love of my life. I'm devastated that we won't get the life we intended to have. I want to spend the rest of our lives together, have children, exotic holidays…"

"I loved you too, Sophie." Tears rolled down his cheeks.

Loved. Past tense. I didn't like the sound of that.

"If you've been watching me, you know how much pain I've been through. I've been trying to work through my grief. Andrea's really helped me through it. Knowing you've come back to tell me you're at peace will really help us all move on."

31

"Move on? I don't want to move on! I'm not at peace. I want to be with you again!" I roared.

His eyes widened with incredulity. "But we can't be together anymore, as horrible as that might be. I have Andrea now, and you're dead…"

"But it could be so, if I entered Andrea's body, and…"

"No!" he raised his voice, shaking his head, already knowing what I was suggesting. "That's not right!"

"But you're only with that bitch as rebound. You know that you could never love her as much as you love me! We are the real deal!" I shouted back.

He let go of my hands, but I quickly grabbed his, caressing the engagement ring he had left on his finger.

"We could still be married. I could permanently inhabit Andrea's body."

He looked horrified.

"No!" he stood up, backing away.

My own face came to the surface, violently appearing in a haze of grey, of bleeding discoloured flesh. His handsome face contorted with horror. I cried seeing his terrified expression. I had expected to be met with love and adoration, not fear and disgust.

"It would be good for Andrea. Her father is dying. She's depressed and has nothing to live for," I tried to reason with him.

"What? She never told me that. Why didn't you tell me that, Andrea?"

I felt her coming forth in a rush of energy.

"I didn't want to burden you with my grief as well as your own." Andrea held her throbbing head, gasping and crying as she tried to force me out of her, her voice managing to break through.

"Oh, Andrea. I want to be here for you as much as you are for me. I feel guilty knowing you've been hurting and you didn't turn to me for help." A tear rolled down his cheek.

"No, no!" I seethed, taking over again, casting a blackness across Andrea's face.

Andrea started to cry hysterically. "*That bitch Sophie didn't...* No, Podge... *ask permission to possess me...* Don't listen to her... *She broke the vase my Dad made me for my 12th birthday...* Podge, I love you... *Please, I just want her out of me. She's crazy!*"

Max was frozen to the spot, horrified at the rapid transition between the two women, the two voices emanating from his girlfriend. Sophie's voice was chilling. Her spirit had become warped.

"This isn't you, Sophie. When you were alive you were never cold. You were a caring nurse who would care for the sick and dying. You would cry at charity advertisements on the television! Sophie, please let Andrea go," he pleaded.

"Maybe I'm cold because I'm dead and everyone has just moved on like I never existed!"

"That's not true and you know it!" Max held his hand up to show her the engagement ring. "I still have my ring. You've been watching me grieve for you.

Why would I do that if I never cared for you?"

"Because my corpse was barely cold and you were already in bed with this slut!"

"How dare you. Andrea is not a slut!"

"She's nothing more than rebound, because you had to do anything to feel close to another human being after my death. I bet you imagined that she was me when you were making love."

Anger overtook Max's sorrowful expression.

"I love you, Andrea. I was feeling guilty at moving on so quickly. It didn't feel right at first, but why not?" He threw his hands up in the air. "Sophie is gone. Dead and gone," he glared, trying to evoke a reaction from Andrea, trying to bring her to the surface.

"I'm not gone, Podge. I'm still here!" My chest racked with sobs. I felt heartbroken all over again.

"*My* Sophie is gone. This freaky, scary Sophie is not the woman I fell in love with."

I was furious. I screamed and ran at him like a demented banshee, bashing him with my fists, scratching him with my nails, and emitting low, dark growls that made him whimper.

"Leave him alone!" Andrea screamed, desperately trying to pull me off him. I staggered backwards, narrowing my eyes, an evil grin etched onto my face. I ran out of the room, clattering down the stairs, sounding like an insane woman yelling at herself as Andrea and I argued.

Max fled after her, following her into the kitchen.

He heard a kitchen drawer being opened, voices babbling on in two different tones. A sound of metal dragging against metal made him wince. The glint of a knife being held up in the air caused him to stop dead in the darkness of the doorway.

"If I can't have you then nobody can." I held a knife to Andrea's face, smiling psychotically. I pushed the tip of the knife into her cheek. It stung. A drop of blood rolled down her face.

"Please, don't..." he whimpered.

I ran for Max, hurling the knife towards him. "We can be married in the afterlife!" I yelled.

There was a heavy *thunk* as the knife embedded itself into the wooden door frame.

Max gasped, pushing me aside, running into the kitchen. He scattered, panicking. It suddenly dawned on him that he was still wearing the engagement ring. He wondered if this had something to do with Sophie being stuck here. He had an idea. He desperately hoped it would work. He turned on the gas hob on the oven. The blue flames crackled as they ignited then turned a deep orange, hissing in the silent darkness of the room.

"You remember those horror films we used to watch, Sophie?"

I remained silent, horrified as he held the ring threateningly above the flaming hob. Orange flames licked at the tarnished gold.

"When the ghosts used to hang around because of an object that still connected them to the earthly world? And once that object was destroyed, the ghost would vanish and leave the living alone?" he grinned, eyes full of malice, his manic expression full of joy.

"Don't do this, Podge. I love you."

"I love you, Andrea."

"Noooo!" I shrieked as he dropped the ring onto the flames. The ring got stuck on one of the metal rods the saucepans are placed on. The alloy began to crackle and melt, blackening in the harsh heat.

At once I realised the ring wasn't even real gold. Just like his love for me, the ring wasn't pure either. The fake alloy was melting like it was plastic.

I began to burn up. It felt like I was on fire, like every part of my soul was burning, leaving. The agony was intense. I screamed in pain. I heard Andrea screaming, too. I felt myself parting from her, her body expelling my sentience, my ghostly essence frittering out and burning in the air like phantom embers.

Max watched on in astonishment, guilt and relief as Sophie's ghost parted from Andrea's body, dying a second death, wailing and contorting in agony as she was destroyed by the flames. The last scream finally rang out, the last wisp of her burning away, and the room was plunged into silence.

The normal sounds of the kitchen came back into focus, the hissing of the ring melting on the hob, and Andrea sobbing on the floor.

Max hurried towards Andrea and threw his arms around her. She cried hysterically, shaking, holding onto his arms. Her hair stuck to her wet cheeks as she buried her face into his chest. He kissed her head and rocked her slowly. They stayed there for a while, sitting in silence, comforted by each other's tight grip.

Max stayed at Andrea's house that night.

* * *

Three weeks later, Max and Andrea were at the hospital visiting her father. Andrea was fussing about him, trying to plump up his pillows and pour him some water. Max placed some flowers in a clear glass vase and then pulled out a brown paper bag from his shoulder bag, holding it by his side.

"I hear that your cancer has gone into remission, Mr. Folcombe." Max smiled at him and then Andrea.

Andrea beamed back at him.

"I am thankful to say so, yes. And call me Rog, lad."

Max grinned again.

"Doctor Emil says I should be able to come back home soon," Mr. Folcome smiled.

Andrea's mother was sitting on a seat next to the bed. "Doctor Emil is very pleased with his progress, says it's a bloody miracle!" she coughed, laughing.

They all laughed, too.

"What's that?" Andrea asked, seeing the brown package Max was holding suspiciously at his side.

"Well," he started to say, placing the package on the bed table and opening it up, pulling out a newspaper, a white ceramic vase, a pot of iridescent glitter, and a tube of craft glue, "seeing as your vase somehow got broken, I thought you might like to make another one. Together."

Andrea squeezed Max's hand tightly, mouthed thanks and kissed him on the cheek.

"That's mighty thoughtful of you, lad," Rog nodded at him and pulled the table over the bed closer to him. Andrea sat next to him on the bed and began to open the tube of glue, smiling at everyone as she handed the pot of glitter to her father. He accidentally tipped it over. They all laughed.

I stood in the room and watched them enjoy making a new vase, a new memory. I had no powers now my physical link to the mortal world had been destroyed. I'd been banished to hover invisibly in the aether, just like before.

It was my punishment.

I watched my Podge fall in love with the woman of his dreams. I watched Podge simpering over Andrea, smiling at his good deeds now he was part of the family. I watched them leave the room hand in hand, snuggling each other as they got into the car. I watched them rarely think about me ever again as they had children and enjoyed exotic holidays together. I watched them live happily ever after for the rest of their long, wonderful lives.

Until the day he died, I watched my Podge.
My Podge.

FILE CORRUPTED

"Of course I've heard of the Akashic Records!" Jacy snorted. "What sort of Native American would I be if I hadn't? The Akashic Records are believed to be a mythical compendium of mystical knowledge stored on a different plane of existence, information encoded onto the aetheric plane, just beyond our reach, infinitely hidden within the aether, pretty much like a universal computer database."

"And it supposedly records all information of every person who has ever existed and every event that has happened throughout human history?" Lucy asked, wide-eyed with fascination.

"Supposedly, yes," Jacy answered. He threw his long black hair over his shoulders and straightened the collar of his leather jacket. He frowned as he tried to wipe a dirty smudge off his denim jeans.

Lucy eagerly knocked back another double shot of brandy. She felt unsteady, probably a mixture of these crazy tales and the alcohol. She smiled woozily at Jacy's older brother, Chayton — Chay for short. He smiled back at her, sheepishly, or perhaps with disinterest. She couldn't quite tell. She'd never met these people before tonight. It was her last day on holiday in West Virginia and she wanted to make the most of her time there. She'd gone into a bar for a drink. Jacy had started chatting her up and she soon found herself in the middle of a strange conversation.

"There's no *supposed* about it. The Akashic Records *are* real," Jacy and Chay's grandfather, Alo, muttered. He was sitting on a stool at the other end of the bar, his hand clasped tightly around a glass of whisky.

"The Assyrians, the Phoenicians and the Babylonians all believed in the Akashic Records — that there were some sort of celestial tablets in existence that contained all manner of spiritual knowledge. Other cultures have envisioned the information as stored in books or in some sort of cosmic library."

"That's interesting. I have read about the clairvoyant Edgar Cayce who used to go into trances and recall his encounters with the Akashic Records. My favourite author, Kevin Tornett, wrote about the mythology of the Akashic Records in his cult classic 1992 book *Esoterica*, and I've been obsessed with all things weird and wonderful ever since. Unfortunately, Kevin died only a few years later, never knowing the full impact of his iconic writings," Lucy said sadly as she leaned up the wall.

"I've not heard of Tornett, but yes, Edgar Cayce was a modern seer. Some have the gift to see spiritual planes of existence that are unavailable to the rest of us, those of us that don't have the gift," Alo explained.

"How would one access these spiritual records?"

Lucy asked, trying not to fall over as she attempted to sit down on a stool next to their sage grandfather.

"Well, if you have to go into a trance to see or access them, maybe you should try that," Jacy offered.

"I can't go into trances, apart from drunken ones!" Lucy laughed.

Alo suddenly looked disgusted, shaking his head.

"Then you will need some help to get into the trance. If you if you know what I mean?" Jacy widened his eyes.

Chay shook his head. "Don't do this, Jace."

"Drugs?" Lucy clasped her hand over her mouth. "I don't know if I could do that."

"Well you'll never see the Akashic Records then, will you?" Jacy shrugged.

"You have no shame. Sharing secrets of our heritage with complete strangers. These things shouldn't be messed with. If someone who isn't meant to see the records accesses them, then they might damage them. If they are damaged then it could destroy all knowledge of mankind. Millennia of information ruined just for the selfish whim of one person," Chay spat, becoming animated.

"I would never ruin anything! I would just view it!" Lucy protested.

"It's too dangerous to consider. Only fools would want to mess with things they shouldn't. I'm having no part of this. Neither should you." Alo got up from his stool and put his hat on. Chay followed him, solemnly, and they left the bar.

Lucy burst out laughing in her drunken stupor. "Your grandfather is very serious!"

"He's the old-school type. He believes all the old tales, and Chay believes everything he says without question. He could convince him that an apple is an orange." Jacy took a swig from his bottle of ale.

"So you don't believe in the Akashic Records?" Lucy raised her eyebrows questioningly.

"Not really."

Lucy felt disheartened. "But if they were real, how would you go about accessing them?"

"Like I said, you'd have to go into a trance, and for that you'd have to take some potent hallucinogens to shift your perception to be able to see them."

"But if they are hallucinogens, what if I was just hallucinating the events?"

"It's not like that. I have read the elder's recipes used for inducing spiritual trances. Here," he took a pen from his pocket and a napkin from the bar.

"Cannabis," he said, writing it on the napkin.

"I can get that."

"And Absinthe."

"Absinthe?"

"Yeah, it contains an ingredient called Thujone which has psychoactive effects."

"Wow, I didn't know that. No wonder perception is altered when drunk," Lucy groaned, rubbing her aching head, thinking how she often drank so many different types of alcohol without realising or caring what was in them.

"Yup." He continued to write.

"You're smart. Are you a scientist or a drug dealer?"

"Neither. I'm a natural herbalist," he frowned. "And Psilocybin mushrooms."

"Magic mushrooms? Oh crap, I've never taken anything like that before. I've never even smoked a normal cigarette! What if this fucks me up?"

"Do you want to see the Akashic Records or not?"

"I do."

"Then that's what you have to take. You have to blend it all together and drink it. The calming effects of the cannabis will coincide with the psychoactive components of the mushrooms and level you off into a trance-like mode."

"And then the records just magically appear?"

"Oh, no. The elders say a chant to get it to work. I'd forgotten about that."

"A chant?" Lucy raised her eyebrows.

"Yes, to gain access. What was it now? Ah yeah, *Umbray, Innay, Untay...*" He scribbled it down.

"You're having me on!" She puffed her cheeks out, laughing wildly.

"I'm not!"

"Have you ever tried this?"

"No, a couple of my friends have, though. Chay has. That's why he's so eager that nobody else does it. Plus grandfather went mad when he found out. Nearly disowned him for doing a forced trance. Chay doesn't have the gift of seeing, so he tried it this way, manually. I don't care, though. You know I'm a rebel," he winked.

"I do," Lucy grinned.

"So here it is: the mere mortal, manual way of gaining access to the Akashic Records. Try it at your own peril." He folded the napkin and held it out towards her between two outstretched fingers.

"Thank you." She took it and placed it in her blouse pocket, patting it securely.

"Another drink?" he asked her, signalling the bar tender.

"Hell yeah!" she whooped.

* * *

Three months later, Lucy found herself in her back garden. She'd continued her normal life, but her thoughts had been consumed by the curiosity and obsession of the Akashic Records. She had always kept her esoteric interests to herself, for the fear of ridicule by closed-minded people, or perhaps rational people. The sceptic in her had been whispering to her that such things were impossible, and she desperately wanted to prove it wrong. She wanted to prove that there was a weird and wonderful mystical side to life.

Lucy stared down at the glass full of blended drugs she was holding and wondered if she was being crazy.

Yes, you are being crazy, her inner voice told her.

"You're having a life crisis! Travelling around America to 'find yourself' isn't the answer. You're right here! Find a job!" her sister would yell at her.

Her mother had been slightly more sympathetic: "You're single and you've been made redundant. You're just going through a bad phase, but things will be okay."

It didn't feel like everything was going to be okay.

Lucy stared out at the trees that lined her garden and the vast field that stretched behind it. Their leaves were rustling in the slight wind, probably laughing at her, just like everyone else did, probably saying, "Look at that loser!" She felt deflated by her own imagination, by her own low opinion of herself. She hadn't wanted to admit to herself, let alone to anyone else, that she was having a life crisis and an emotional meltdown, but it was happening in full force. This quest for the fabled Akashic Records had been a welcome distraction from her own feelings.

"I'm thirty-three and I have nothing going for me. No job. No partner. No hope. My life sucks. Screw it. What do I have to lose?" Lucy often talked out loud to herself. She didn't have anyone else to talk to.

Her modest garden in England seemed like an unfitting setting for an unearthly event, but at least it provided some sense of familiarity and safety.

"Shall I really do it?"

Lucy clutched nervously onto the glass full of thick brown mixture. It had been surprisingly easy to acquire the ingredients she needed. It had taken longer to muster up the courage to actually do it. She took a deep breath, feeling the impending foolishness if this crazy mission didn't work. She was ultimately more worried about her health, hoping she would be okay with the effects of the drugs. If she passed out, would any of the neighbours see her and help? If she died, would she be lying here, rotting in her own garden for the next six months before anyone even noticed? She shuddered, peering around, seeing that nobody was around.

"No. Everything will be fine. You always assume the worst!" she scolded herself. She shook the negative thoughts from her mind. "Here goes. Bottoms up!" She poured it into her mouth.

She nearly vomited it straight back up, but she did her best to hold it down. "Errrgh!" she cringed at the acrid taste. The thick, gloopy texture made her gag as it refused to go smoothly down her throat. "Man, I should have blended it more." She took one final gulp, feeling foolish and disgusting, and it finally went down.

Her head soon became woozy and she felt like she was going to pass out. She instantly felt out of it, like a tight rubber band was squeezing her head. Her vision flashed in different colours, oscillating and rescinding until everything became stable again. Her head became clear again.

"Wow, that's disgusting." She almost choked again at the awful taste in her mouth. She stood there nervously, staring around the garden.

Everything looked normal. The same as usual. The mental fugue had passed quickly. Too quickly. It didn't feel right.

"Why do I feel normal? I don't feel any different!" She screwed up her face, wondering if something had gone wrong. "A total waste of £150," she sighed, thinking she could have put that towards another holiday. She threw the glass to the floor and it smashed on the concrete tiles that bordered the lawn.

Then she remembered. "The chant!" She took the napkin from her pocket and spoke the words on it, probably mispronounced. "*Umbray, Innay, Untay...*"

A strong wind came from nowhere, whipping through her hair, rustling through the trees, interrupting the previously calm afternoon. A magical feeling tinted the air. Foreign tongues chattered excitedly in the breeze.

"Oh, wow!" she gasped as she stood in her back garden staring up at the metaphysical sight before her.

The Akashic Records.

It worked!

It had actually worked!

She stood at the base of her garden, right next to a hexagonal paving stone which was now glowing blue. It appeared to be the base point of access. Somehow she had accessed the part of the archive which stored a complete collection of every human being who has ever existed. A seemingly unending number of semi-translucent ghostly figures stood motionless in a line that arched round in a spherical queue, stretching as far as the eye could see along the landscape, across her garden and the field beyond.

This spiritual archive was nothing like she had expected. She had imagined it to be an ethereal exploration of endless layers of information rather than the structured and methodical, and all too solid record that presented itself. Chaotic and infinite levels of information that would be all at once too much for the human mind to handle, yet this record looked ordered, methodical. There must be a higher order to its completion and containment. She considered that it might appear differently to the perception of each person that accesses it. That's why some imagine it in book form or like a library or a computer. Hers seemed to be different; it was in human form.

There didn't seem to be any apparent order, just hundreds of people from various eras in all manner of dress, projections of every single person who has ever existed. There was a pale, staunch-looking Victorian woman in a high-collared black dress, frozen to her spot, a half-naked Aztec man in brightly coloured cloth staring blankly, unmoving; a myriad of all the sorts of people you could possibly imagine — old, young, fat, skinny, healthy, diseased, and everyone in between. It was incredibly overwhelming to see the never-ending line of unrecognisable faces.

She found it unimaginable to comprehend that she had the chance to potentially meet and talk to anyone who has ever lived, those who were long dead, to meet and converse with the greatest philosophical or scientific minds in history, to uncover remnants of great mysteries, political figures, historical dignitaries, Neanderthals, and no end of brilliantly ordinary folk.

Somehow, as soon as she thought about the line moving, it began to scroll, each person moving onto the hexagonal stepping stone.

Stop, she thought.

The rotation suddenly stopped. A frail old man stood hunched before her, clutching onto his walking stick so he didn't fall, his watering eyes blinking, his breath rattling in his chest. Lucy gaped at him, unnerved by the vivid quality and solidity of his body compared to the ethereal figures neighbouring him.

"Who are you?"

"Henry Tattershall," he rasped. "Where am I?" he asked, peering around in confusion.

"Umm..." she grimaced awkwardly, unsure how to answer. She thought about scrolling, and so it set off again. Henry was gone. A few others came into solidity as they passed by.

Lucy gasped as she saw someone she recognised nearly halfway down the garden. She suddenly felt giddy with excitement. She scrolled fast until he landed on the stone.

"Wow!" she exclaimed, feeling her cheeks flush, absolutely astonished. "Leo Walden, my favourite actor!" she gushed, unaware until now that it also included everyone currently living as well as dead. She'd had a crush on him for years and couldn't believe her luck. At twenty-eight years old, he stood at nearly six feet tall. A fine stature of a handsome man in his prime. Dark blue eyes twinkled under the sweep of his sandy brown fringe. He stood with his weight on one leg, hands in his jacket pockets, the epitome of cool.

"Hi," he broke the ice. "Who are you?"

"Lucy."

"I'm Leo…"

"Walden. I know. I'm a huge fan," she blushed.

A wide pearly grin made her melt as he reached out to shake her hand. She quivered as she returned the embrace, pulling him into a hug.

"Nice to meet you, Lucy," he winked. His reputation as a rampant womaniser wasn't failing him. She felt herself flush.

"You look and feel so real." She couldn't take her eyes off him, wanting to squish his arms to check he wasn't just a projection.

"I am real," he smiled, peering around the garden. "Well, I am real, in a way. I exist as a biological projection of this archive."

Leo put a step forward, taking his foot off the paving stone. They both held their breath, waiting for something catastrophic to happen, like the wind to rip them apart, but nothing happened.

"I don't think you should leave the line..." Lucy's voice trembled, the elder's words of caution echoing around her mind, intensifying her worry.

Leo ignored her plea and took another step

forward, leaving a vacant space between two people. "It seems okay," he said, peering behind him, swallowing hard.

"Okay," she breathed out heavily, trying to relax herself. "Will you stay for just a little while?" she pleaded, fluttering her long eyelashes at him.

"I suppose," he smiled coyly. "But not for too long! We'll have to be quick..." he flirted with her.

She couldn't believe her luck. Leo Walden was actually flirting with her!

Her coy smile fell from her face as she glanced back at the wheel to see her favourite author, Kevin Tornett, standing about five people down the line. He was standing there motionless. Her jaw dropped. As she had explained to Jacy, Chay and Alo, she had first read about the mythology of the Akashic Records from his cult classic 1992 book Esoterica and had been obsessed with all things weird and wonderful ever since. Unfortunately, he had died only a few years later due to a short illness. His work had greatly impacted her view of the world and of life. It was an honour to get the chance to meet him. She scrolled along the line until it selected him.

Lucy sighed in equal excitement and exasperation. "I can't believe it! Nobody of interest appears for some time and now two at once!"

She glanced at Leo, into his alluring eyes, and then at Kevin, standing there in all of his brilliance. Kevin squinted through his glasses at the sunlight breaking through the clouds, becoming amazed at the feel of the wind on his face.

"Oh!" he exclaimed, dropping to the ground to feel the grass between his fingers. "Oh, I am alive again. Thank you! Oh, thank you! You have no idea how amazing it is to re-experience living sensations again." He stood up and hugged Lucy tightly.

"Mr. Tornett, it's an honour to meet you! I have so many questions to ask you." She revered her admiration for his work and the sadness of his passing.

Worry flitted through her as she realised there were now two files removed from the archive. But again, no consequence or damage seemed to erupt. Perhaps Alo had been too worrisome.

"Leo and I are going to hang out for a while. Maybe you should momentarily get back on the wheel?" Lucy asked Kevin.

Kevin's face went ashen. "No! Please don't make me return to the records just yet. Please don't deny me this chance to feel solid earth again, to smell the flowers and to feel the breeze on my skin. I will just stay here until you return. Please!" he cried, in a state of euphoria at being alive again.

Her heart dropped when she saw his distraught expression.

Leo winced, holding his stomach in pain as they chatted. Lucy hadn't noticed and he hadn't wanted to interrupt their conversation.

"What do I do?" She so desperately wanted to chat to Kevin about all of the mystical musings in his work and to find out what he was like as a person before he died. She would never get another chance. But then there was Leo, her favourite actor who she had an insatiable desire to get to know. Someone she doubted she could ever get to know any other way. Both desires for knowledge and lust were equally as powerful and overwhelming.

"Please let me stay!" Kevin begged.

"Okay, you can stay, but don't leave the garden," Lucy suggested.

"I won't. Thank you!" Kevin sank to his knees.

Lucy and Leo headed off arm in arm towards her house, leaving Kevin to stare up in wonder at the rolling clouds.

Lucy giggled as she led Leo into her bedroom. She felt like a born-again teenager sneaking a boy into the house. "What do you wanna do?" she asked, meeting his eyes, knowing full well what she wanted to do, but trying to portray some semblance of innocence. A thought that nearly made her burst out laughing.

Leo grinned slyly, as if he had read her thoughts. He curled two fingers under her chin, tilted her head upwards and leaned in for a kiss. Overtaken with live for the moment passion, she pushed him up the wall to kiss him, opening his shirt buttons, running her hand up his bare chest. They were barely able to contain themselves until they fell down with a thump onto her bed.

Wow! This is really happening! Lucy thought to

herself, feeling smug.

Leo ran his fingers through her long, dyed black hair as she lay on top of him, kissing his face, then his neck, then his chest, then his stomach. He whimpered, but not from pleasure, as he glanced sideways to see his left arm beginning to tear apart like a rag doll. The wound was glowing an ephemeral bluish white. The same coloured bioluminescent substance started to trickle from him like blood.

"Oh, my god!" Lucy shrieked.

He pushed her away. "Please, I need to go back on the wheel. I'm disintegrating!"

Her face contorted. She stared, aghast at his skin and muscles tearing apart. "What's happening?"

"It's probably because I've been off the wheel too long. I'm only part of the record. I'm not even technically real," he said, hand clamped on his arm.

"What do you mean? You feel real to me."

"Well, the real Leo is out there, somewhere," he said, pointing a finger towards the wall in a figurative direction. "I am metaphysically assimilated with him, a mere reconstruction of his existence. I'm not the real person. I guess it's unnatural for me to walk the earth the same time as him. I thought it would be okay, but obviously it's not!" He clutched his side and cried out in agony.

Lucy placed her hands on his chest in an effort to comfort him but quickly withdrew them as his whole body throbbed in a luminous bluish white light. He returned back to solid colour. The colour had drained from his face and tears rolled down his cheeks.

"I knew I shouldn't have come off the wheel just for a quickie. I knew that a woman would be the end of me!"

"You think that's bad? I've gone off the rails! Lately I've been drinking heavily, taking psychedelic drugs and trying to have casual sex with a projection of my favourite actor!" Lucy cried, feeling hurt.

Leo groaned. "It's so weird. I know what Leo thinks, how he acts. Yet I am not him, just a shadow copy that grows into a larger file the more experiences he has."

Lucy felt guilty for messing so recklessly with fragile material. "I'm so sorry. I don't want to corrupt Leo's, erm, your record by disintegrating him, erm, I mean you... God damn it!" she cried, burying her face in her hands.

"We're both to blame. You need to put me back on the wheel before it's too late!" Leo winced as he sat up, grasping her arms tightly. "I didn't think of it before, but everything Leo has done since I have been off the wheel, and is doing right now, won't be recorded at all. Every menial detail is vitally important to a person. Every action, every thought, every decision, every feeling has to be recorded so he has a whole record. All of these elements shape his life and define him as a person, and I have corrupted that!" He zoned out and stared into the air, disgusted with himself.

"Quick, get up. Let's go back to the wheel." Lucy

helped pull his shirt around him. He grimaced in pain as he stood up. She put an arm around him to steady him. She felt horrible about what was happening, trying to take in all the information he had just given her.

"What about Kevin?" Lucy asked as they left the bedroom and hobbled down the stairs. "Will he be okay?"

"Yes, physically, because he's already dead, but his life record has already been completed. He's lived all the experiences he was meant to live while alive. But new data is being added from this post-death experience which doesn't belong in the record. We have corrupted the records either way."

Lucy felt numb with fear. The elder had been right. Only fools would mess with things they shouldn't mess with. She had never felt so foolish.

Leo gasped in horror, placing his hands upon his stomach. His torso had begun to tear apart, sparkling blue goo oozing between his fingers like a rush of blood. Full of panic, Lucy put one arm around his shoulders and one around his waist, holding him for support. They struggled out of the back door and towards the garden.

"I'm so sorry. I should have listened to the Native American elder. I've used this spectacular technology for my own selfish gain," Lucy cried. She hadn't even had the chance to scroll through her deceased relatives and loved ones. Instead, she had blindly followed her impulses. She had ruined the possibility of seeing their faces again, of hearing their voices once more, if only for a moment.

They both shrieked as they exited the back door of the house. A strong hurricane-like wind blew into them, nearly knocking them off their feet. Lucy squinted, holding up a hand to her face to stop the sheer force of the wind. Her long black hair whipped around her head. She saw countless figures rotating rapidly on the spot. The file corruptions had caused some sort of manic auto-scroll to take control.

"Argh, what the hell?" Lucy shouted as the high winds began to rip into the garden, plants and earth, whirling large mounds around in the air. The pair desperately tried to hobble towards the glowing access point in an attempt to get Leo back onto it.

"My location has gone by!" Leo yelled, clutching his sides. The wheel was rotating at a high speed. The people whizzed by faster and faster, turning into a motion blur. A flash of blue-white light appeared every second a figure passed through the access point.

"What's happening?" Lucy shouted at Kevin. He had clamped onto the metal fence pole of the washing line, hanging on for dear life. They struggled against the force of the wind to get back to the hexagonal paving stone.

"I think that the software has initiated a forced shut down because we've corrupted the data. We've ruined the Akashic record of the whole of mankind. It's destroying your world while it's at it!" Kevin shouted, trying to be heard over the raging wind.

"What have I done?" Lucy cried, feeling an immense guilt weighing down on her shoulders. She had been fortunate to glimpse a spiritual technology, and would no doubt have to pay the price for this ungodly damage of epic proportions.

"Get back on the wheel!" Lucy motioned at Kevin, pointing towards the mark, hoping their rejoining it would somehow quell the damage. He managed to steady his feet on a jutting floor tile, and then leapt towards the mark. He overshot it, but the wind blew him backwards right onto it. He disappeared in a bright flash of blue light.

Lucy and Leo edged against the remaining fence panels until they were adjacent to the mark. She could barely see as her hair wrapped around her face. Unable to prise her hands away from the fence, she spat her hair out of her mouth, apologising again to Leo, even though he could barely hear her over the raging wind.

Managing to release one hand, she pushed him forwards onto the mark. He also disappeared in a bright flash, but it was too late. The mark started to suck everything in like a black hole. The landscape was disintegrating and spinning around the mark like a vortex. The wind was too powerful.

Lucy couldn't fight it any longer. Her hands released their grasp on the fence. She let out a terrified scream as her body got pulled towards the mark, trying to grasp on to any upturned objects as she was dragged into the vortex. Her fingernails scraped through the dirt before she was left clutching the air in mid-flight. Lucy's screams suddenly became silent. An immense, blinding flash of light momentarily illuminated the garden as she was sucked in completely.

Everything went still and quiet again.

It was all over.

The paving stone remained where the point of access had been located, surrounded by a several mile-deep crater where the land had been devoured by the vortex.

Everything was now silent and calm. The malfunctioned technology had imploded and destroyed itself completely.

The Akashic Records were no more.

Lucy was no more.

The human race will just have to remember itself.

THE HAZE

Jennifer held the white plastic stick of the pregnancy test in her hands. She stared at it under the artificial light, hoping somehow that the result would change. But it didn't. She was definitely pregnant.

"Holy shit," she gasped. The stick dropped from her grip and landed on the floor. She threw the toilet cubicle door open and rushed over to the sink. Her stomach was doing somersaults. Thinking she was going to be sick, she gripped the plastic basin and stared into the mirror.

"Oh, my god, I'm pregnant," she said, confirming it out loud. A wave of hot panic washed over her. She ran a hand through her sweaty red hair. With jagged, heavy breaths, she sobbed until she could barely breathe. She tried to force herself to calm down. She turned on the tap and splashed cold water on her face, hoping it would somehow disguise her bleary red eyes.

She couldn't hide it for long. She would have to tell Tom.

"I'm only eighteen. I'm not ready to have children," she sobbed, shaking her head. "I'm still at college. What about my career? I don't even have a job! I can't afford a baby. What am I going to do?"

Things were moving too fast. Tom was her first boyfriend. They'd only been dating eight months and she'd already moved into his flat with him. She'd wanted to prove to her parents that she could be independent. But lately she'd been questioning her choices. She loved Tom, but the weighty prospects of the future and adult responsibility were daunting.

Was he *the one*?

What if he wasn't and she was tied to him with a child? She hadn't dated any other men to find out. It felt like too much commitment at such an early age. She wanted kids one day, when she was older, but not right now, not at this age. Plus, they weren't even married. Her dad was the old-school type who assumed that everything should be done in order: dating, marriage, and then children. He was going to go nuts.

A thought entered her mind.

I could get rid of it.

She shook her head, feeling ashamed. Her auntie had tried so desperately to have a baby, spending years and huge amounts of money on IVF, with no success, and Jenny had just got pregnant without any effort. It just didn't seem fair.

It was an accident.

Another hot wave of panic and distress washed over her. She ran out of the door of the public toilet and dashed straight past Tom.

"Jenny! Wait up. Where are you going?"

She shook her head, not answering him.

61

"Jenny, wait!"

Her feet thudded onto the gravelly road below. She quickened her step down the empty stretch of country road. Dry grass fields neighboured the road on either side. The extraordinarily hot summer sunshine streamed down onto her pale, freckled skin, making her wipe her sweaty brow. Even her tiny green shorts and black halter neck top offered no relief. Curly flame red hair bounced up and down on her shoulders as she walked as fast as she could to get away from him.

Tom finally caught up with her. He placed a hand on her shoulder and spun her around. His expression softened when he saw that her eyes were red from crying.

"Jenny, what's wrong?"

"Leave me alone!" she cried, pushing him away.

"Jenny. Why have you been crying? Please tell me what's wrong!" He took hold of her again.

For a moment, Jenny stared at Tom, searching his dark brown eyes as if trying to predict his response. She looked him up and down. He was wearing shorts, trainers and a loose-fitting tank top that showed off the slim and athletic physique he'd been working on. A section of his dark brown fringe fell down to his eyes, catching on his eyelashes as he blinked. Tom was handsome, but still had a boyish face. He was only eighteen too. Jenny felt foolish. Thoughts of fear and worry consumed her.

We're just children pretending to be adults. How

can we bring up a child properly when we're still children ourselves?

"Jenny?" Tom asked carefully, tearing her away from her thoughts.

"I'm pregnant."

The shock set in and the colour drained from his face. "What? No way!" He released his grip on her.

Not giving him chance to process the news or even chance to properly respond, she took off, running down the road. She had no idea where they were. They'd gone on a random walk down some country lanes, and luckily, she'd found some public toilets, giving her chance to try the pregnancy test she'd been too scared to take.

Tom trailed half a mile behind her, shouting for her to slow down. But in her usual hot-tempered manner, she just wouldn't listen.

"I just wish I could disappear!" she cried, tears stinging her eyes. "I can't face this situation. I just want to get away from all this."

As soon as she thought she'd got far enough away from Tom, something caught her eye at the side of the road. A blistering wave of heat rushed through her, making her feel like she'd walked into an oven. She stopped suddenly, feeling light-headed, like she was going to pass out. Heat waves simmered up from the barren fields. They looked nearly as dry as the lump in her throat. She stood still, staring at the hazy clearing, which somehow didn't look right. There was a section of the air where the waves rippled upwards intensely in one area in a unified formation, unlike the rest of the road.

"What the hell is that?"

Mesmerised by the haze, she moved closer towards it. She noticed that they weren't heat waves at all, but very thin crystallised layers of colour. Colours which didn't seem to reflect the brown and green of the field behind it, but overlapping multi-coloured hues weaving through a translucent haze. Hues that were moving.

Jenny waved an arm through the haze, pulling it back quickly. It felt cool. It made her skin tingle, but it didn't hurt. Curiosity overwhelmed her and she decided to walk through it. She stopped dead in her tracks as she realised she was suddenly somewhere else entirely. She shivered. The temperature was suddenly a lot cooler and the sky was a lot darker. Day had become night. Summer had become winter.

The surroundings had an unnaturally dark tint. It felt like even moonlight would be afraid to fall here. She appeared to be on an abandoned field, but it looked different to the field she'd just been on. She began to walk across an unmaintained concreted floor area, which had started to break up due to weathering over time. Tall, unkempt grasses sprouted up through the cracks. Ruins of demolished buildings lay around her, parts of walls and corners still visible amongst the crumbled structures.

She wondered where she was. Even though the air was still and there was no breeze, a chill came over her. Her teeth chattered. She shuddered, huddling her arms around her body, feeling like she would never get warm again. She turned around to face where she had just walked from, but she was just met with the sight of the field.

No haze.

No rippling colours.

No Tom.

Panic set in, causing her to walk backwards and forwards through the space, hoping the haze would somehow rematerialise from the aether and allow her to return to where she came from.

The atmosphere unsettled her as she noticed there was no breeze. Nothing was moving at all. Stagnant, like the place was frozen in time, outside of time. There was no sound, no activity, no comforting rustling of trees or chirping of birds. She whimpered in distress as she looked up. Dark ominous clouds sat there in the sky, not moving an inch.

Jenny realised this place was abnormal. Everything was suspended, as if time had been displaced. Entropy and causality had no effect here. The haze appeared to be an anomaly. An anomaly she had walked straight into. She felt so stupid.

"What is this place?" she spoke. The words whipped from her mouth. Her voice surprised her. It sounded metallic, tinny, as if it was being carried along on an invisible wind that she couldn't hear or feel. She winced. It sounded so horrible.

Feeling lost and confused, she walked through

the jutting stone remnants of the ruins. Part of a broken plaque lay on the floor. She gasped when she saw the inscription upon it. "Dobson's College. Built 1964," she read aloud. Her tinny voice grated on her.

My college! she thought. She wondered how it could it be derelict like this when the college was still standing, still active. But its location meant she was close to her parent's house. Miles away from where she was before she had walked through the haze.

Wait, what year am I in? she thought, not wanting to hear her unnerving tinny voice again. She realised that she would have to be in a future time for the college to be knocked down.

She desperately wanted to get out of this weird void. How much time had passed since she'd been here? What felt like half an hour could be decades in the real world.

The real world...

She almost laughed at how ridiculous that sounded. A fear panged at her heart and her head started to heat up as she tried not to imagine the possibilities. What if she couldn't simply walk back to the time and place she'd walked in from?

I know I wanted to disappear, but this is weird.

A bright and hazy light suddenly flooded her vision. Straining her eyelids open, she could see small spherical blobs of light. An unnerving high-pitched, metallic ringing pierced the silence. She cried out in pain, clasping her hands to her ears. It went on for a few agonising, never-ending seconds until it fell dark and silent again. She breathed a sigh of relief, trembling from feeling so frightened and fragile. The blobs started to crystallise, this time in larger wavy lines of moving colour. It was a welcome dissonance against the foreboding backdrop.

The haze!

She took a step forward but then hesitated, wondering what sort of reality or time she would next encounter. But she had to move. She couldn't stay here. Her body tingled all over as she pushed herself through this new haze.

The atmosphere had changed again. The first things she noticed when she stepped to the other side was how dreary and grey everything was: the dismal wet weather, the dull mood, the dull atmosphere. Life in general seemed solemn and bleak here. The dewy air was cool but a lot warmer than the chill of the haze. At least nothing sounded tinny like in that strange void. There was breeze now. There was movement. There were people!

"Finally, back to civilisation. But where am I?" she asked aloud to herself, pleased her voice sounded normal again. The crumbled ruins of the college had gone, had been rebuilt upon. Across the road there was now a huge grey building. Its grey triangular roof panels jutted into the dreary grey skyline. 'Dobson's Academy. Built 2018. 20 years of technical innovation!' was inscribed onto it in darker grey lettering.

That would make the year 2038.

Her head span as she tried to contemplate what had happened. She'd somehow walked twenty-five years into the future. She placed her hands on her flat stomach. Her child would be twenty-four in this time.

Filled with fear and curiosity, she started the journey to where her parent's house would be, meeting a few dead ends and newly created roads until she recognised the right street. Her parent's house came into view. She breathed a sigh of relief. Luckily it was still there.

She walked down the dreary street, which now had a cobbled floor and grey buildings. The future air felt different, softer. She passed a small, rounded brick bridge on one side of the road and a row of small houses on the opposite side. She walked up to the steps to the front door of her parent's small terraced house. Everything had changed so much. This was a whole different time, a whole different world.

She knocked on the front door.

No answer.

A few long minutes passed and she wondered what to do. There was a flat, grey plastic panel on the front door. With curiosity, she opened the flap and saw a screen with an image of a hand printed onto it. She hesitated before instinctively placing her hand on it. The screen felt soft like foam. A red light scanned her hand, making her jump back in fright. The residue off her hand soaked into the foam. Red dots came to the surface forming the words 'DNA match'.

"That's weird."

She heard a click as the door unlocked. Security had certainly been stepped up in the last twenty-five years. She entered and looked around the house. The decor had been changed and the furniture was different.

"Hello?" she called out.

Still no answer.

A red light flashed silently in the corner of the room. She wondered if it was part of the security system.

Feeling dehydrated, she took a bottle of milk from the fridge, swallowing huge mouthfuls from it as she walked through the house. There were many recent photos of her in frames, decorating the fireplace and the walls. Unfathomable technological gadgets lay around the room. There was a stainless steel dome on a table with a small flat circular button on its roof, lined with a blue light. She pressed the button and a convex image made from light suddenly shot up from it. The image showed a scanned newspaper cutting.

Tuesday July 24th 2018

Eighteen-year-old Jennifer Taylor went missing last week during a walk with her boyfriend, Tom Stanton. Stanton claims that Jennifer announced she was pregnant and then simply vanished. No body has yet been found. Stanton claims his innocence but is currently being held as a suspect. Jennifer's parents and the police are appealing for

witnesses or any information regarding her whereabouts. In the case that Jennifer has run away, Mr and Mrs Taylor have stated emotionally: "We miss you with all our hearts. Please come back home, sweetheart."

Jennifer couldn't believe what she was reading. This was horrible. Feeling distraught and finding it hard to breathe, she ran outside. She stopped dead in her tracks.

"No, it can't be..." she gasped, putting a hand to her mouth.

Three people had emerged from the far right, on the opposite side of the road. She instantly recognised her father's bald head and limp, and her mother's back-combed hairstyle, although her red hair was now grey. They looked older, but even from this distance, she could tell it was her parents. They were with a man she didn't recognise.

There were quite a few people around as she stood on the front step, staring down the street, watching the three people get closer.

When they got close enough, they all stared at each other intensely, bemused and too overwhelmed to speak.

"Mum? Dad?"

She dropped the milk. The plastic bottle bounced, a splash of milk erupting from it.

"Jennifer?" They finally broke the long silence, shock etched on their faces. She bounded over to them and hugged them both. They all started to cry.

"Jennifer. You've actually come back to us," her father cried.

"Where have you been?" her mother finally managed to say through heavy sobs.

"I don't know..." she replied genuinely. She glanced over at the man who was with them, the man who was staring at her in horror, and realised who he was — her boyfriend Tom! She hadn't even recognised him. His black hair had flecks of grey in it. He looked dishevelled. Deep lines had collected under and around his eyes and he had a haunted look about him.

"Jennifer? No, it can't be you. How is this possible?" He looked frightened, like he had seen a ghost from the past. Quite literally.

"Our Jennifer has come back home to us!" her parents cried, wrapping their arms around her.

"But how? How do you look exactly the same as the day you disappeared?" Tom squeaked, staring at her youthful teenage face. His voice was deeper now, different. "You're even wearing the same clothes." Her hair was long and wavy and she was slim, everything they remembered her to be. Her parents let go of her, staring at her.

"I..." She wasn't sure how to answer.

"How have you not aged? Where did you go? Where have you been?" Tom's voice became more aggressive. Her parents were staring at him in silence. She swallowed so hard that it hurt her throat. The rain became heavier, battering down onto them. She was cold and shivering. The cold air bit at her bare legs and the rain had soaked through her flimsy summer wear.

"About twenty minutes ago… I mean, the day I went missing… I was walking down a country lane. I saw a strange haze in the air. It looked like heat rising from a radiator, rippling through the air. Curiosity got the better of me and I walked straight through it. I ended up in an abnormal, strange void. I walked out again and now I'm here."

They stared at her like she was insane, but they couldn't deny the evidence standing in front of them. She hadn't aged a day past eighteen.

"You've been missing for twenty-five years." Tom's voice cracked with emotion, a mixture of resentment of her going missing and joy that she was back.

"I can't explain it."

"The police thought I had murdered you, Jenny."

The bitterness in his voice made her eyes sting with tears. "I just read the newspaper clipping about my disappearance on that light thing in your house."

"The HoloDome? That old thing still works?" her dad asked, eyebrows raised.

"Um, yeah." It was all too much to take in.

Her parents stared inquisitively at her, flabbergasted.

Jenny began to think how she had lost out on a huge portion of her life. She'd always been scared about growing older, but now she reckoned that the only thing worse than growing older was missing the chance to. They were old, she was young, and all was lost. She had never felt happier than to be reunited with them, yet a deep sadness rang through all of them. She started to cry. "All these years... And you still see each other. I'm so pleased." She could barely see out of her teary eyes.

"We were devastated when you went missing. We pulled together because that was the only thing we could do," her mother answered, her voice trembling. "We didn't want to believe that Tom had murdered you."

"That's because I hadn't," he snapped.

Her dad placed a reassuring hand on his shoulder. "We thought you might have run away. But when you never came back, and we never found your body, we just didn't know what had happened to you."

"You never moved?" Jenny motioned a hand towards the house.

"We stayed here with the hope that you might return one day. We never lost hope. We couldn't. That's why we installed the DNA security alarm. We couldn't believe it when the sensor was vibrating and flashing in my pocket. I've looked at this device every day for the last twenty-five years, wishing and hoping it might go off, but nothing. Until today. Today is the day it finally went off," she sobbed, pulling a handkerchief from her pocket and rubbing her wet eyes with it. Jenny's father put an arm around her

73

mum in an attempt to comfort her.

"Oh, mum," Jenny wept. Her face was wet from the rain and her crying.

"And you…" Jenny turned to Tom." Did you find anyone else? Get married?" she asked, her lip quivering as it hurt too much to consider him being with another woman, but at the same time she had hoped that he'd moved on. Hell, she hadn't moved on. He was still the love of her life only half an hour ago! She felt guilty for the feelings she'd felt, that she even questioned her love for him when she knew how good to was to her, and how much he loved her. Now she felt like she loved him more than anything, the young him, anyway. She didn't recognise this older man standing before her. This stranger. How much he'd changed.

She felt angry that she'd been robbed of her loved ones and the chance to be with them. It also felt as if she was mourning the loss of herself. She mostly felt that way because she could see the sadness within them, in their eyes, the sadness that they had endured for years. It didn't seem right or fair that a bizarre half an hour should pass for her while they had suffered two and a half whole decades of pain. But now she was feeling it full force.

Tom finally answered, breaking their silent musings. "I have dated a few women but there's not been anyone special. I could never commit to any of them. I could never find anyone like you. I could never love anyone like I loved you. I have lived with the hope that you would somehow come back to me, to us..." he said sadly. "And now you have!" he beamed, but the smile quickly fell from his face. "Although I expected you to look a lot older."

"I'm back now!" she said optimistically, weakly, taking his hand in hers.

"You still look young, so young, and I look so old. You're still a young woman. I'm now a middle-aged man. It can never be as it was. It's not right. We're not the same people anymore." He shook his head.

"I'm still the same person." Stunned, she blinked tears out of her eyes.

"That's the weird thing. You haven't changed one bit, and we've changed dramatically. Of course we're glad to have you back. I just don't see how we can continue as before. The world has changed. We have changed. We don't understand what has happened here!"

She stood in silence, trying to figure out what to say.

"Why did you leave us?" Tom suddenly became animated, angry. "That day... You told me you were pregnant. You dropped that bombshell on me then ran away, never to be seen again, until now. I had the chance to be a father, a husband. I thought you'd run away and left me, or worse, I thought you'd committed suicide."

"This isn't my fault. It was the haze. I can't explain any of this!" she sobbed. "I didn't run away…" she swallowed, feeling guilty, because that's exactly what she had done. She'd run away from her problems without a second thought for how her loved ones would feel. She'd abandoned the people who loved her more than anything. She felt so selfish, but she wondered why she was being punished so harshly, so cosmically for a moment's rash decision.

"I spent years thinking your disappearance was my fault," her father piped in. "I thought that because I was always so strict with you that you would fear my response. I worried that you'd gone missing because of me. But we never found your body. I lived with the hope that you might somehow be alive, that one day you would return to us. Of course, I was shocked that you accidentally got pregnant at a young age, but I would never have hated you for it. I would never have abandoned you. I would have supported you. You're my only daughter. I love you."

"Oh, Dad. I was so scared. I am so scared." Jenny buried her face in her hands.

Her mother put an arm around her, trying to console her. The rain had begun to bait. She could hear a dripping sound as the rain trickled from the canopy of the house and into a puddle below.

"I just want to go back and change everything."

A bright light suddenly took over their field of vision, a bright haze that resembled the sun shining down after rainfall. She turned to face it, feeling the warmth of the bright white light shining on her face. But it wasn't sunlight. It was the haze. It was flowing upwards from the ground in one area. The light dimmed, revealing translucent watery-looking waves of colour.

"The haze. It's here."

They all stared at it, mouths agape.

"I don't know what this *haze* is, but maybe, maybe things don't have to turn out this way," Tom secured a look at her.

She knew at once what he meant, to try to find the right time to return back to, back to the time she went missing.

"But what about you? If I go back, what happens to you all?"

"I don't know. If we exist here, we'll still be miserable. We'll still be lonely. But we're used to it now. We accept it. At least we'll know you're still out there. But if there is a chance that you can find the right time and wipe this timeline out, overwrite this bleak, grey future and make everything right, as it was before, make us completely unaware of you going missing, then go for it. I wouldn't want anything else. Make the old, I mean young me happy again," Tom explained. "I don't want you to know the miserable, broken man I've become. I want you to be with the young, loving man I used to be."

Jenny cried at his sacrifice, that he was so wise and willing to give her up again for a better future, past, a better life, the life that they had. How she had greatly underestimated the man she loved. She'd never even given him chance to prove what a great partner and father he could be.

She turned back to them. "I will. I love you all."

"We love you too. Thanks for coming back home," they sobbed. They embraced one last time, not wanting to let go. They gaped incredulously at the magnificent sight before them, watching her as she walked into the wall of light, watching her disappear almost as soon as she'd arrived, losing her again after just getting her back.

"Goodbye," she said, not turning around to face them as she left.

The waves of the haze crystallised into chunky hexagons of colour. She could see colours and shapes moving within them, but she couldn't make out details. It was like looking outside through mottled stained-glass windows. But they weren't grey. These weren't the hues of the colourless future.

Nobody else seemed to be able to see the haze but the four of them. The light enveloped her body and she could see nothing else but light, feel nothing else but a cool warmth that made her body tingle as she stepped into it. It felt like she was floating as she lifted her leg forwards. She closed her eyes as the light filled her vision and a discordant clanging noise filled her ears. This time, however, it was a soft tone, pleasant almost.

As she emerged from the haze, she expected to meet hard gravelly ground, but she didn't. The ground was smooth and flat. Wherever she was now, it wasn't the day she went missing. There was no blistering heat, no open fields, no Tom.

She opened her eyes and was met with the sight of a market square. The landscape was filled with different sized futuristic-looking buildings.

The haze had gone.

"What the hell?!" she started to cry in fear and frustration. She was no longer wet from the rain, but it was cold here, and the sky was beginning to get dark — the cusp when daytime turns to evening.

"Where the hell am I now?" she huffed, feeling exasperated. She traversed the square and walked past a huge white building. White triangular roof panels jutted up into the cloudy skyline, lit up from beneath with multi-coloured neon lights. A hologram was being projected into the air: 'Dobson's Academy. Built 2018. 70 years of technical innovation!'

The words made her feel faint.

Not knowing what to do for the best, she did what she did before and headed in the direction she thought her parent's house was situated. She hoped she was going the right way, but everything looked so different. A lot of change can happen in seventy years.

"Seventy years... Seventy years..." she kept repeating to herself as she walked, shaking her head in dismay. She trundled past a small yard. There was a tall woman collecting clothes from a washing line. She looked middle-aged but still had quite a youthful face. Her brown hair was tied up into a bun, and she was wearing a woollen cardigan, a loose dress, and slippers. She looked comfortable and homely. The woman turned and smiled at her. She looked familiar.

Jenny smiled back sheepishly, weakly, wondering where to go next or what to do.

"Mum! Dad just called from the academy." A young teenage girl bounded outside, holding a strange contraption in her hand. Her long wavy brown hair fell down to her waist. She had beautiful olive skin and a messy fringe that got in the way of her large brown eyes.

"He said that..." The girl turned to face Jenny. She stopped dead in her tracks, staring open-mouthed at her.

"Yes, Camille?" the tall woman answered, a bundle of laundry rolled up in her arms.

"That he's staying later at work tonight..." she trailed off, staring in shock at Jenny.

Jenny felt unnerved by the girl's deep stare. She peered at the older woman for an explanation.

"What's wrong?" the mother asked.

"She looks just like Great Nanny Jen when she was young."

Great Nanny Jen? Jenny felt a deep uneasy feeling in the pit of her stomach. Given that, her instinct told her she could trust these people.

Camille bounded over to the fence and opened the wooden gate. "Come in. You must come in!" she said to Jenny.

"What are you doing?"

"Don't you see, mum, how much she looks like Great Nanny Jen? Look at her!"

The mother strained her eyes due to the darkening sky, but then a realisation suddenly hit her, and the same bemused expression as the daughter came over her face.

"I do see. Oh, my days. You do look exactly like her. Please, come in from the cold," she said, inviting Jenny inside.

"Thank you." By this point, Jenny felt too numb to protest or even think straight. She'd travelled through time twice in one day, and she was finding it difficult to fathom. She'd finally thought she was returning back to her own time, but had ended up even further away.

"My name is Sara and this is one of my children, Camille."

"I'm the middle child. I'm thirteen. I have an older sister, Beatrice, and a younger brother, Tommy," Camille explained enthusiastically, nodding.

"My name is Jennifer," Jenny mumbled.

Sara raised her eyebrows. "Jennifer?"

"Jennifer Taylor."

Camille gasped, putting her hand to her mouth. "Just like Great Nanny Jen. The exact same name!"

"But Great Nanny Jen's surname was Stanton, not Taylor." Sara shook her head.

"Taylor was her maiden name, before she got married." Camille stared at Jenny, looking her up and down in disbelief.

Jenny would normally scoff, but after the weirdness of today, they could indeed be her future relatives. She stared at them, trying to look for any genetic similarities. Could these people really be her future family? In this future, she must have had the baby.

"Enough," Sara said, ushering Jenny into their modest lounge area. It was filled with more technological, futuristic gadgets of which she had no idea of their function. "Please sit down," Sara said, motioning towards a table and chairs.

"Thank you," Jenny said, gingerly sitting down onto the hard chair. She felt woozy and she felt like she could be sick at any moment.

"Would you like a drink?" Sara asked.

"Please," Jenny croaked. Her throat was so dry.

Sara went into the kitchen and came out with a glass of water. She placed it on the table in front of her. Jenny quickly drained it. She hadn't realised how thirsty she was.

"You look really pale," Sara said. "If you don't mind." She placed a flat stick against Jenny's head. When she pulled it away, it had the words '42 degrees' flashing on it. "Your temperature is very high."

"But I'm so cold," Jenny shivered, sweating.

"I think you have a fever."

"I am having a rough day," Jenny said weakly.
Understatement of the century.

"You seem lost and confused. Are you okay?" Camille asked, looking concerned.

Jenny shook her head.

Camille and Sara wouldn't stop staring at her. Camille was holding something in her hand, a bunch of what looked like photographs.

"What are they?" Jenny asked.

"Don't bother her with those!" Sara snapped.

"But she looks so much like Great Nanny Jen! The hair, the eyes, everything! They even have the same name. It's so bizarre. I just wanted to show her." Camille jumped up and down, fervent with excitement.

"It sure is a weird coincidence," Sara said calmly, but her bewildered expression betrayed her.

Jenny smiled at Camille as she took the photographs from her. She seemed like a nice girl.

Camille smiled back eagerly.

Jenny couldn't believe her eyes. It *was* her in the photographs. She flicked through her baby photos, holiday snaps, even selfies she'd uploaded to the internet.

"It is me!"

"What? How?" Sara asked.

"I knew it!" Camille clapped her hands together.

"No, that's impossible! Anyway, Great Nanny Jen is dead," Sarah sighed.

Camille looked sad. "I loved my Nanny Jen, but I was only a baby when she died."

"I'm dead?" Jenny said in a panic. She rifled through the photographs in a wide-eyed stupor. She didn't recognise most of them because she was older in them, at various ages ranging from birth to death.

She was posing with people she didn't even know yet, but there were photos with Tom — their wedding photos, photos of an older her with Sara and Camille, an older girl and younger boy she assumed to be Beatrice and Tommy, and many other unknown family members. A pictorial documentation of her life, the life she hadn't lived yet. The life that had come and gone by, like the other time slip, a life she hadn't experienced.

"When did I die? How old did I live to? Who are all these people? I want to know! No, I don't want to know my future. I feel sick." She placed a hand over her mouth.

"Uh, oh," Camille said, racing away. She quickly returned with a bucket, which Jenny promptly vomited into. She sat there shivering. "I'm so sorry. This is all too much."

"You can't be Great Nanny Jen. It's impossible."

"She has to be. I know she is. How did you get here? Did you time travel or something?" Camille asked.

"Yes... somehow... I walked into a haze and ended up in some weird future times." It sounded so simplistic. It sounded so insane.

Sara was staring at her in wonder, fascination and trepidation. Sara was becoming increasingly startled, unable to shrug this whole situation off as a weird coincidence.

Jenny was still shivering. Camille fetched a jumper and handed it to her.

"Thank you," Jenny said, putting it on. Camille pressed one of the buttons on the sleeve and it suddenly began to warm up as if it had heating installed within it.

"Woah, how is this warming up so much?"

"It's just your standard Heatie," Camille shrugged.

"A heated jumper? It feels like I'm wearing an electric blanket."

Camille laughed. "A what? The fibres are thermal, but they're controlled by the temperature buttons. There's low, medium, and hot. I love them in winter. I have Coolies for summer, too. The latest fashion designers are trying to combine the thermal functions of both into one garment. I dunno what they're gonna call it though. It started in blankets and then moved onto other pieces of clothing. It's just basic fabric temperature regulation." She nodded as if that explained everything.

"She's only so obsessed with it because great grandfather Tom invented it."

"He made a fortune!"

"Tom..." As fascinating as future technology was, Jenny had gone back to staring at the photographs. She found a photo of herself around the age she is now, a lovely photo of her and Tom holding a baby. Her lip started to wobble. "I have the baby? We look so happy."

"You're pregnant?"

Jenny nodded. "I only found out today."

Sara patted her hand, seeing how terrified she looked. "You'll be okay. Seriously."

"I'm worried I'm too young to be a mother. I'm only eighteen."

"We all think that. I thought that I was too young when I found out I was pregnant with Beatrice and I was twenty-six! It's normal to be scared. You find a strength you never knew you could possess and you just get on with it."

"You look happy in the photo. That's Nanny Tanya when she was a baby," Camille added.

"Tanya? I have a girl?" Jenny sniffed, smiling. With her chubby face and big grin, Tanya looked like the cutest baby girl ever. She'd always wanted a girl. She'd always loved the name Tanya, too. It seemed plausible.

"Yup. And she had mum."

"My mum died last year," Sara said, a sad expression taking over her face.

"I miss Nanny Tanya. She used to give me SucklePops, but my mum won't let me have them," Camille glared at Sara.

"I just don't want your teeth to rot! Plus they're dangerous. Lollipops with exploding sherbet is silly. It's unnecessary. Exploding sweets should be banned." Sara folded her arms defiantly.

"It's only a small plume when you open the wrapper. They're fun!"

"Tell that to uncle Dave when one exploded up his nose. He was sneezing sherbet for a week. His nose hasn't been right since!"

"He always predicts when he's going to sneeze before he does. It's his party trick. I call him Nostrildamus!" Camille roared with laughter.

"You are a funny girl!" Sara gave in and burst out laughing too. Camille went over to Sara and hugged her.

Jenny watched them talking, bemused because she had no idea what *Heaties*, *Coolies*, or *SucklePops* were, but she saw how happy they were and she felt guilty for even thinking about getting rid of the baby. These people wouldn't exist if she got rid of baby Tanya. Even though she was terrified, she'd had a glimpse of a far future world. It sounded like she was going to have a happy life ahead of her. Perhaps things would be okay after all.

But then what of the experience where she'd gone missing and not had the child? It was a total contradiction to this timeline. Which one was true? Which one was real? Was it all up to her to decide?

Of course it is. My decisions dictate my future. She felt herself flush, taking the Heatie off.

All of a sudden, a strange haze began to appear in the room. It was rippling and undulating like before. It twinkled in a myriad of colours, twisting and turning into pretty and mesmerising kaleidoscopic shapes.

"Woah! What the hell is that?" Sara and Camille got up, staring at it.

"It's the haze. It's returned. It's my portal back home."

"You really have travelled from the past?" Sara finally confirmed her doubt.

"Please don't go!" Camille cried, hugging Jenny tightly.

Jenny placed an arm around her and kissed her on the head. "I wish I could stay longer and get to know you all better. It's been amazing to meet you both, but I must go. This isn't my world. This isn't my time."

"Yes, you must go," Sara said, hugging her tightly. "I spent a lot of time with you throughout my life. You're an amazing woman. You'll be an amazing wife, mother and grandmother. I know this first-hand."

Jenny sobbed, staring at a quote on a plaque on the wall. "True happiness is to enjoy the present, without anxious dependence upon the future," she read quietly. It seemed so apt.

"I'm already proud of you both," Jenny smiled, tears rolling down her cheeks.

"Love you, Nanny Jen," Camille cried.

"Goodbye," Sara breathed in deeply, squeezing her hand affectionately.

"Goodbye."

Jenny tentatively stepped through the haze. Even though it was the prettiest haze she'd seen, its motion was far from pleasant. The movement was so turbulent, racking her this way and that, that she hadn't even realised she'd passed out.

"Jenny. Jenny, wake up!" she heard Tom's voice.

She came around. Tom was standing over her.

The hot sunshine was streaming down onto them.

"Are you okay? I ran down the road and found you passed out on the floor. Have you hit your head?"

"No, I don't think so," Jenny said, feeling the top of her head with two fingers. There was no wound. "I'm back! I'm back! Oh, Tom! I've missed you so much." She wrapped her arms around him and hugged him like she never wanted to let go.

"We've only been apart a few minutes."

"It feels like much longer," she sobbed.

She stared around looking for the haze, which was now gone, but was met with the sight of dry fields and countryside foliage. Everything was bright and colourful. She was dry now as if a spot of rain had never dropped onto her.

Tom's face was youthful once again. She admired his pale, unblemished skin, his gorgeous eyes and his lovely soft, dark hair. Free of age lines and misery. Free from the grief and hardships of possible futures. What a beautiful sight he was.

"Oh, Tom! I love you so much."

"I love you too."

He was surprised when she pounced on him and hugged him tightly, never wanting to let go of him again, kissing his face over and over again.

"This wasn't the reaction I was expecting. You seem delirious. Maybe you passed out because of the heat or... or because... I can't believe you're pregnant! What are we going to do?"

"Whatever we do, we're going to be fine. I'm

sure of it." She thought of the quote on Sara's wall. "True happiness is to enjoy the present, without anxious dependence upon the future."

"That's very philosophical of you," Tom frowned. *Very delirious...* he thought.

"Who knows what the future will hold. All we have is now."

"Are you sure you didn't hit your head?"

"I'm sure!"

She frowned, thinking of the two contrasting scenarios she'd experienced — one where she'd run away, or worse, ended her life, and the alternative of having a loving family, generations of wonderful people who existed because of her.

Was it possible for both scenarios to have happened in different future timelines? Or were they metaphorical to her situation? Did the haze produce these alternatives especially for her as some sort of massive metaphorical, metaphysical creation of her inner turmoil? Or had she passed out and imagined the whole thing?

But I distinctly remember walking through the haze...

"I can't believe I'm going to be a dad. I'm so happy." Tom was grinning from ear to ear.

"You are?" Tears spilled down Jenny's cheeks.

He nodded and put his forehead on hers, kissing her on the nose. "This is a huge commitment. We both have to agree on this."

"I think we have to take responsibility for our

actions." Getting pregnant had been an accident, but it didn't mean it was a mistake.

"Is it what you want? Do you want a baby right now?" he asked, his tone serious.

She stared into his dark brown eyes. She'd already made her decision somewhere in the haze. It felt like she'd lived several lifetimes in the span of an hour or two. It had made her feel stronger and wiser and had brought a clarity of thought. She nodded. "I do. I'm just terrified."

"Me too. But we have each other."

"We do." A warmness filled her and she placed an arm around his waist.

"Let's go home," he said, putting an arm over her shoulder.

Her happiness to be back in the present moment took priority over her fear over her metaphysical encounter. As they walked down the country lane, she thought of the people in the future, pondering upon the possible outcomes from her decisions. She wondered if they still existed or if they would ever exist now. Had she changed the future or had she just chosen a different timeline? It seemed ironic that she was now the one plagued with the memory of someone from a distant time instead of her descendants.

But none of that seem to matter now she was in the arms of her loved one, in her present time. Back to the time in which she could make decisions rather than the memory of her life being laid out to her.

Whatever they chose from this point onwards would be their decision. The haze had shown her all the possibilities.

Now had never seemed so beautiful.

She tried to hide her face as she cried tears of joy because she had a second chance at her own life. Her wonderful life that thankfully she'd not lost. She was eighteen again and had her whole life ahead of her.

"As I was telling you earlier, I had a crazy idea for an invention," Tom enthused. His comment tore her from her weighty pondering.

"What was that?"

"About controlling the temperatures of fabric. It'd save a fortune on heating and air conditioning."

Jenny couldn't believe it. Had she imagined it from Tom mentioning it earlier and incorporated it into her vision of the future or was the future actually coming true?

"My mate Donny said it was a stupid idea."

"No. It's a brilliant idea! I reckon you should patent it. Perhaps you could call the hot ones Heaties and the cold ones Coolies."

Tom laughed. "Daft names."

"Cute names. Cute sells. As for me, I'll be waiting for SucklePops. They sound fun."

"What?"

"Exploding sherbet lollies."

Tom scoffed. "You are delirious."

Jenny smiled to herself. She would never walk through a haze again.

THE PHOENIXIS

"Nature is resplendent in all its biological glory. The marvel of the seed pod, nourishing the tender seeds within, bearing them like fruit, a shell that hardens, shrivels and perishes. It protects the seed from the harsh elements of nature and predators until it is ready and strong enough to take form. Its biology has evolved to a flawless design of distribution. When the time is right, the pods split open to scatter or drop the seeds into the soil. The dying shell harbours the potential for such vivid life within. That one tiny seed can then take root and flourish into a beautiful plant, a huge tree or thriving shrubbery."

Peter raised an eyebrow, wondering what this had to do with the fabled Phoenixis.

"There are other things in nature which displays the cyclical motion of bringing new life into the world: the caterpillar battling to emerge from its cocoon, the baby bird struggling to peck its way through its protective eggshell, much like how the womb enriches the foetus in love and nourishment.

And just like the Phoenix, The Phoenixis is also consumed by fire and rises from the ashes reborn. Life is borne from death and death can only come from life — the never-ending cycle of causality and nature."

Peter tutted, shaking his head. "Such fancy words. Someone is taking the literary metaphors too far."

He took a swig of ale and continued to read.

"The fabled Phoenixis resembles the elements of his namesake, the Phoenix, and like the aforementioned elements, from decay he is reborn afresh. He is certain that a mother must have given birth to him. How else could he exist? He prefers to imagine it that way anyway."

"How the hell would they know what I imagine?" Peter narrowed his eyes, feeling taken aback by the webpage he was reading. He looked at the browser title. "Portland's Local Folklore, by Sarah Summers," he read aloud. He ruffled his hair, leaning back in his computer chair.

Peter was a fabled Phoenixis, and he didn't appreciate Sarah's imagined account of his life and transformation.

"She's got some of it right, but most of it's bullshit. She doesn't know the actual process involved, and I don't even turn to ash. I certainly don't burst into flames!" He drained the last mouthful of beer from his bottle of ale and threw it into the bin under his desk.

He winced at the crude sketch of a Phoenixis, probably drawn by Sarah herself. A man with wings looking pleased with himself, a bunch of ash on the floor around him.

He snorted. "Oh, please, as if it's that easy. Plus,

it looks nothing like me!"

He carried on reading, now in a mocking tone. "Even though he is technically an astounding creature, the 'creature' is part of the problem. He wishes to be solely human. Considering himself a biological anomaly is a hardship that has plagued him since his existence. The Phoenixis is only a name given to him by local folklore stories."

His heart dropped.

"Way to make me feel even more insecure. Thanks, Sarah." He shook his head, closing the browser.

"I need to get out of the house," he said to himself, kicking his chair back, getting up and stretching his arms up into the air.

Peter had been holed up in his house since his last transition. His transitions always arrived suddenly and excruciatingly at sporadic times. If only it would stick to a routine, say once a month, so he could at least plan life around it, but no such luck. The process drained him of energy for weeks afterwards.

"Hello, world," he said as he threw the front door open, taking a deep breath. He collected his mail and newspaper from his front porch. Portland was a gorgeous place to live, especially in the autumn. Peter lived in a rural area near to the woods. The perfect area for a recluse like him to hide away from prying eyes. He sighed at his meagre mail. Apart from some manuscript documents, it was mostly junk mail from local businesses and fast food joints. It was hard to find work in the community being a Phoenixis. That's why he worked from home as a freelance editor. His occasional clients at the other end of the computer didn't know or care what he looked like as long as he did a good job.

When it was shedding time, he would just hole himself away at home until he was fully reborn again.

Peter sighed. He hated his lonely life. If only he wasn't cursed with such an unstable yet regenerative bodily gene then he might be able to make some friends. Maybe even a girlfriend. He laughed at the thought. It was preposterous, but his heart panged with loneliness and emptiness.

A noise caught his attention. He looked up to see his neighbour across the street. Mandy. She was doing some gardening. She looked over, as if she had sensed eyes upon her.

"Hey, Peter!" she waved at him, beaming as she pulled off her gardening gloves and threw them down onto the lawn. She proceeded to walk across the road to chat to him.

"Hey!" Peter waved back.

"Not seen you for a while. When did you get back from travelling?" she asked, leaning on the fence.

Her shoulder-length blonde hair was tied up in a messy ponytail. Half of it had come loose while she was busy trudging around with a wheelbarrow.

Peter liked how she had a stocky body, strong arms from hard physical work and a steely demeanour that showed she wasn't to be messed with, but she had kind eyes and a loving smile that put him at ease. Mandy was a salt of the earth kind of woman who didn't mind mucking in, hauling logs around and getting her hands dirty to help anyone out.

Peter smiled. He felt comfortable in her company. He thought she was brilliant.

"Travelling?" he suddenly asked, tearing his mind away from his considerations.

"Yeah, not seen you around for quite some time. I noticed your mail piling up on the porch. Didn't know whether to collect it for you or not 'til you returned." She blew her sweaty fringe out of her eyes with an upturned bottom lip.

The last shedding time... Peter realised.

"Oh, yeah, I went to Canada," he lied.

"Ooh, it's nice there. I wish I could afford to go on holiday every once in a while. I hope you had a nice time," she remarked warmly, without a hint of jealousy in her voice.

"Yeah, I did, thanks. I went hiking and canoeing and whatnot." At least those were the activities on a Canadian tourism poster he had pinned up on his wall. He hoped she didn't ask any more questions that could unveil his dishonesty.

He grinned, nervously rubbing the back of his neck. He suddenly felt self-conscious about his image. He lived in a constant state of paranoia. Was his condition already beginning to show?

No, it's not transition time yet.

"Busy?" he asked, nodding towards her garden.

"It's autumn. It's always hard work to maintain the grounds for winter and prepare it for next year. And then there's harvesting the seeds, drying out the herbs... Ah, you know, rural life." She rubbed a smudge of dirt off her cheek.

Peter nodded.

Autumn reminded him of his condition, everything dying off and preserving the momentum of regrowth, as Sarah had so eloquently pointed out on her blog. Luckily, he was fine at the moment, in both body and spirit. His normal body wasn't too bad to look at. He had vaguely handsome features, normal anyway. Short, greying hair, light brown eyes, a slim body with a comfortable stomach roll. He didn't think he was a catch but he felt he had something to offer and surely wasn't the worst.

Average Joe. That suited him just fine.

Perhaps he could be friends with Mandy during the times when he wasn't in metamorphosis. When it was regeneration time, he could always just go 'travelling' again for a while. A surge of confidence suddenly rushed through him.

"Hey, Mandy, do you fancy hanging out one evening? We've been neighbours for years now and I've never invited you around for dinner."

Mandy looked surprised, her raised eyebrows lost under her thick blonde fringe. "Sorta like a date?"

Peter shrugged then nodded his head agreeably. "Yeah."

"Sure, then. Not like I've been waiting for you to ask…" she chuckled. "I sure get lonely rattling around my large house with only my dogs, my bees and my chickens for company. It'd be great to have some human company now and then."

Human. The word rattled around his head.

"Brilliant. How's about tomorrow night? I could do a barbecue." Peter's face couldn't contain his grin of excitement. He'd spent so long alone that he too desperately craved some human interaction.

"Tempting me with a barbecue!" Sounds great to me. Why wait 'til tomorrow? What about tonight?"

Peter's stomach flipped with nerves. "Tonight is fine."

"Cool. What time do you want me round?"

"Eight? Nine?" he asked, unsure of the best time for a dinner date.

She sensed his nerves and applied a reassuring tone to her reply. "Around eight will be fine. I'll bring some wine, and beer." She coughed. "Ah, I'll drop the lady-like pretention. I can drink pints like a navvy!" Her already pink cheeks flushed crimson.

"Well, I look forward to it!" Peter said more enthusiastically than he meant to. He was trying to play it cool after all.

"See you later then, Pete," she said, somewhat girlishly, which seemed out of character for her. She nodded in acknowledgement, then headed back to resume her gardening.

"See you later!" Peter called after her. He took

his mail into his house. He closed the door behind him and punched the air in celebration.

Animated by his uplifted mood, he began to clean the place up. It had become unkempt during his last transition. He had so much preparation to do for the night ahead.

"I have a date! An actual date with an actual woman!" he smirked to himself. He couldn't believe he'd actually asked a woman out on a date. All of that worrying and putting it off for so long had only made him more hesitant. If only he had asked her before.

"This place looks like hell," he said, walking into the kitchen. Pots and pans were everywhere. Housework was hardly a priority during transitions. He started to sweep the floors. He couldn't stop scratching as he cleaned. At first, he thought it might have been a reaction to the bleach he'd used, but the familiar feeling of his skin drying began to set in.

"Noooo!" Peter cried as he ran over to the mirror. The first symptoms of regeneration were appearing. Dry blotches of skin like severe eczema made him itch furiously.

"No, not again! My last shedding has only just finished!" he yelled, slamming his fist against the wall.

Panicking, he ran upstairs into his bedroom. There was no way he could let Mandy come around now. There was no way she could see him like this. By tonight, he would be the most hideous sight.

"Why me? Why am I so cursed?" He picked up a

glass and threw it against the wall. Glass smashed everywhere. Furious, he upturned the bedside table. The lamp rolled across the dusty floorboards.

"The moment I even try to make friends and this is what happens. How could I have been so stupid to allow myself to try to forge a relationship with another person? I hate being me! I hate this stupid body!" He slumped down to the floor and covered his head with his arms.

Hours passed by as he sat on his bedroom floor in desolate torment. For hours, he sat staring blankly into space. The darkness of the approaching evening overtook his room, plunging him into a moonlit dusk. The glare of the luminous digits on his digital clock hurt his eyes. He watched them change to 19:45. He was worried why his shedding transitions were becoming more frequent and sporadic. Could it be his emotions affecting his biology? Speeding his cells up to react quicker?

The sensation of desiccation was at first more uncomfortable than painful. In only a few hours, the condition of his skin had degraded considerably. His smooth flat skin was now a flaky discoloured grey, thickening into a scaly dermis.

All of a sudden, he heard a knock at the front door.

Mandy knocked on the front door.

No answer.

She stared up and around at the windows. The

place was in complete darkness. She knocked again. An excruciatingly long minute passed as she stood waiting with awkward impatience, waiting for him to open the front door. She tapped her foot impatiently, wondering whether to go back home or to knock again.

Her heart dropped. "You're a complete fool to think a man would actually like you, Mandy-Jane," she sighed as she clutched onto the bag of goodies she had brought with her; a gesture of goodwill — beer, snacks and some board games. She knocked again a couple of times. "Peter?" she called out.

Still no answer.

Hesitantly, she trotted down the front steps. An uneasy feeling pressed her to look up at the upstairs window. "I'd never forgive myself if something was wrong and I didn't tend to it," she convinced herself, deciding to head around the back of the house.

Mandy peered through the kitchen window.

Nobody was there.

Feeling like an intruder, she tried the handle on the back door. It creaked open and she hastily entered, nervously peering around the dark room.

"Peter?" she called out through the house.

A wave of intense, pure panic rushed through Peter when he heard Mandy's voice echo around his old shack of a house. His skin began to crack from being so dry.

"Ugh!" he groaned as he pushed himself up from

the floor. He didn't want Mandy to see him in this state. Nobody had ever witnessed his transformation. Peter would be locked up or killed if anyone knew that The Phoenixis was more than just a tale of folklore.

It was a reality for him.

Large flakes of decaying skin began to fall off and land on the floorboards. More than anything he hated the smell of rotting flesh, only made worse by knowing that it was his own. How cruel of nature to subject him to the process of decomposition, a process that no living being should have to endure or be aware of how it feels.

He fought every urge to vomit, taking a deep breath to combat the smell, closing his eyes to avoid the disgusting sight of his own necrosis.

"Peter?" Mandy called again. The floorboards creaked beneath her as she stepped cautiously through the dark hallway. Her breath was shallow as she looked around for the light switch.

Peter managed to get up. His vision was becoming blurry due to the decaying matter overtaking his eyes. In an effort to hide away, he knocked over the footstool at the end of his bed, tumbling towards the bedroom door.

"Shit!"

"Peter! Are you upstairs?" Mandy shouted up to him before running up the stairs to investigate.

"No, don't come in!" Peter cried out in panic and

fear as he heard footsteps approaching. "I don't want you to see me like this!" He winced in pain as he leant against the doorframe.

"Why? What's wrong?" Mandy walked into the room, not seeing him at first. She turned to see Peter and dropped her bag of beer bottles onto the floor. "Oh, my god," she mouthed, not being able to draw her eyes away from the horrific state of his flesh. Her eyes strained against the dusky light as more details came into focus. He looked like a zombie. Her heart thumped in her chest, and her legs twitched as she considered running back through the doorway.

"It's my affliction. Please, just leave!" he yelled at her, crying and sobbing because it felt like all the nerves in his body were on fire as they began to die, new ones beginning to reproduce in their place. Cells bubbled through and over. Shedding like a snake.

"Your affliction?" She was unable to draw her eyes away, taking a step closer. Mandy was made of stronger stuff than anybody realised. This felt almost like when she would watch cows and horses giving birth. It was a stomach-churning sight, yet something so wondrous and beautiful.

"What's wrong with you?" she asked.

She jumped as he roared out in pain, sobbing hysterically as much as his eyes would allow him, his chest heaving as he tried to draw bigger, jagged breaths.

"I am a Phoenixis," he managed to say. "I am reborn from my own ashes, so to speak. I need to get out of here." He stumbled forwards, heading towards the stairs.

"Peter, wait!"

But Peter didn't wait.

Wanting to tear at his own flesh, wanting to rip his own skin off, he ran down the stairs, clattering towards the open back door, and ran out into the night.

Mandy could hear her dogs barking as she finally got the courage to run after him, cringing as she saw the dead tissue matter stuck on each floorboard where he had stepped. She followed the trail to the backyard and then ran through the dark woods after him.

Her heart was pumping and sweat was pouring through her clothes. The only comfort came from the cool night breeze that ripped through the trees as she ran. She grimaced, seeing a panel of ripped skin hanging from a branch. Peter must have run this way.

Peter was unable to cry any longer, his tear ducts disallowing it, restricting his agony to within as he stumbled through the trees towards an open clearing. Placing a hand on a tree to propel himself forward, he suddenly came face to face with a couple of teenagers making out.

He hated to see the horror on their faces as they stared at him, the stark realisation in their eyes turning from disbelief to fear. They didn't see the man, Peter, they saw a monster. And he didn't blame them.

The girl screamed as her eyes fell over the fetid freak, skin blackening, rough like tree bark, crystallising into a malignant cocoon. His cries of pain rang through the trees like a wounded animal, a tortured beast with a frightening croaky call.

"The Phoenixis! You're real!" she cried. "I wrote about you on my blog!"

"Sarah?" he cried. His voice came out as a terrible, unearthly monstrous roar.

"H-how does it k-know my name?" she stammered. Sarah fell to her knees, her lover half catching her with shaking hands as he kept his eyes locked on Peter. If only they knew he had no desire to hurt them.

Peter trundled away, trying to find a secluded spot to wait out the night in hopeful safety.

"Peter?" Mandy called out as she ran, following the chunks of deceased matter strewn every yard or so across the foliage. The sounds of crying and animated voices filtered through the trees. She followed the sounds and came to the shaking teenagers. The girl was crying, her face burrowed into the guy's chest.

"What's wrong?" Mandy felt stupid for asking when she already knew the answer.

"There's a monster in the woods, ma'am," the guy replied, his voice trembling.

"The Phoenixis! It's more horrible than I could ever have imagined. Its skin. Oh, its skin!" Sarah's eyes were wide with terror.

"The *what*?" Mandy raised her eyebrows, not that they could see her properly in the darkness.

"Please tell me it's gone. We need to get out of here!" Sarah cried.

"We need to tell the sheriff. We need to alert the groundsmen. Someone. Anyone!" the guy said.

"I'm tracking Pete... The Phoenixis," Mandy corrected herself to avoid suspicion. "The creature ran that way, so follow the path in the direction I came from and it will lead you out of here," she pointed.

"Thank you. Be careful," the teenagers said, before making a quick exit, hurrying away.

Mandy sighed and followed the trail of flesh again. "What the hell are you doing, Mandy-Jane? You should be running away in the same direction as those kids. Your mother said you could never keep out of trouble," she muttered to herself breathlessly. She travelled as fast as she could, trying to navigate between the trees and avoid tripping on any upturned branches. The woods were pitch black, trees looming like dark figures, containing the foreboding wind that whipped through the branches.

"Good job you know your way around these woods," she mumbled, pushing herself over a large, twisted root. There was a squelching noise as her foot landed in something sticky, something fleshy. Part of Peter. "Ugh," she grimaced.

The stitch in her side made her pant. She stopped for a moment, gasping for welcome breath. The sound of rustling leaves in the distance urged her to continue her expedition. She took off again. Being a rural girl, she had gone on many hunting and fishing trips with her father and two older brothers. Over the years, she had become quite expert in the art of tracking.

Peter was starting to feel his body being cocooned by the protective layer of dead, hardened dermis as the new flesh rippled and bubbled underneath. Two opposing forces both impacting his body and mind simultaneously.

He wished he could die.

He wanted to die.

He wished he could end the pain. He knew he could endure it, but he wished he didn't have to. He held onto the knowledge that the pain had an end. In a few hours he would be reborn and would feel better than ever, if only for a short time.

He knew the perfect spot to hide. There was a cave at the back of Breckon's Beacon. The rough terrain put most people off going there in the day, let alone at night. Using all of his energy, he pressed onwards, straining to move his limbs against the extreme force of thick extraneous membrane. He felt like a big log hulking through the woods. He suddenly felt at one with the trees, sharing their bark-like exterior.

Almost there now.

His arms and legs cracked as he reached the cave. It was so dark here. Hardly any moonlight filtered through the densely populated trees.

Peter thought how this was the perfect place for monsters such as himself, haunting the woods at night, scaring the wits out of horrified by-passers. It didn't matter to him that it was dark. He could barely see at all anyway now his hardened dermis had begun to eclipse his face. He followed the feel of the tread underfoot, using the muffled sounds of the stream trickling near the cave as means of navigation.

For a moment, he thought he could hear a distant voice.

"Just damn graffiti in the caves. Hardly worth me coming out here at night for. I'd rather be kicking some proper criminal's asses!" the cop spoke into his radio, shining his torch along the interior of the cave wall. "Damn kids ruining nature as usual."

Peter stumbled into the opening of the small cave.

"What the hell?" the cop turned, his flashlight illuminating Peter's rotting, bark-like body.

Peter panicked, feeling mistaken to think that the woods would be empty. Even at night, there was always someone lurking around. Peter tried to call out to warn the cop, but instead, it came out as a ferocious roar because of his constricting throat.

"Holy fuck!" The cop jumped in fright, staring up at the sight of this unearthly wood monster. He wondered if it was some sort of Pagan God come back to life to reclaim the woods, or a scientific experiment that had escaped into the wild. Either way, he thought that something like this had no right to exist, especially not in his jurisdiction.

Cocking his head like a blind dog, Peter tried to turn his head in the direction of the voice, but it was hard given his dry, cracking frame. His jagged, animalistic gestures unnerved the cop. The cop swerved around him and managed to get by the cave entrance. Peter took a big hulking step towards him. They emerged outside of the cave into the clearing.

"Stay back!" The cop immediately drew his gun and cocked it. He glared, still shining the torch on him. Although his voice and hands shook in fright, he managed to keep a steady aim on the wood monster. Trying to keep his nerve, he removed his radio, pressed on the side button and spoke unevenly into the receiver. "I have captured, an, uh, monster in the woods."

"What? Could you repeat that, please?" a distorted voice crackled from the other end.

"I've caught a damn monster in the woods! Some sort of wood creature!" the cop shouted.

"What are you talking about?"

"Send back-up immediately! I'm at Breckon's Beacon," he yelled. "What the fuck are you?" he roared at Peter.

But Peter was unable to answer. His mouth cracked into a painfully small hole as he tried to speak, resulting in another guttural roar coming from his throat. He thought about Mandy. As much as he wanted to die, he wanted to live. He pleaded silently with the cop not to shoot him, but he knew the man wouldn't be able to understand. His intentions were lost in translation as he moved forwards to try to run away.

Scared for his life and shaking with fear at seeing such an unnatural creature, the sheriff holstered his radio, took aim and fired straight at Peter's torso.

"No! Don't shoot! He's my friend!" Mandy screamed as she finally advanced into the clearing near the caves, seeing Peter and the cop engaged in a peculiar standoff.

But it was too late.

The shot rang out and embedded straight into Peter's thick bodily cocoon. Peter stumbled backwards, roaring like an injured beast.

The cop took aim to fire again.

"No, don't! You'll kill him!" she screamed.

Before the cop even had time to turn around to see her, Mandy instinctively rammed her shoulder into him and they both went flying down to the rocky ground. The gun clattered from his hands and the bullet got lost within the trees.

There was a muffled *clunk* as the cop's skull met the hard earth. He'd been knocked out cold. Mandy whimpered as she got up. A pain shot up her arm, making her clutch it protectively. She checked to see if the cop was still alive. Blood oozed from his injured head. He was unconscious but was still breathing and had a pulse. Mandy groaned, pulling his dead-weight from the hard ground and onto the softer grasses at the base of the trees.

"Hermie, you there?" a voice echoed from the radio.

She unhooked the radio from his belt. "Officer down, just past the clearing in Breckon's Beacon. Tripped over a branch and hit his head. Get medical care here immediately."

"Who is this?"

Mandy turned the radio off and returned it to his belt. He should be all right, she hoped. She was just glad he hadn't hit his head on the rocks instead of the ground. It would've been game-over for Hermie.

Peter was struggling to get up, a last-ditch attempt to make it to the caves so he could stay there and regenerate overnight. This is why he always chose to transform at home, alone.

"Peter!"

Mandy rushed over to his aid, helping him up. His thick, dark, woody skin felt like rough bark as she placed her hands on him to steady him up. Strangely, she didn't feel repulsed.

He motioned towards the opening of the cave.

She understood, helping usher him inside to safety, unable to take her eyes off his bizarre condition. She didn't feel scared now. She knew that Peter was underneath it all. And Peter was her friend.

She breathed heavily as she helped him fall down onto a flat part of the cave floor. She flopped down next to him, sitting in the darkness, listening to the wind stirring outside. Leaves rustled ominously and nocturnal animals frolicked and hunted outside. The small stream trickling beside the cave was soothing.

Peter groaned.

Mandy shook her head. She now had the chance to attempt to rationalise the peculiar events of the night. She couldn't believe that such biological anomalies existed, 'monsters' that the rest of the world remained ignorant and oblivious to. She wondered what else lurked out there in the aether that she didn't know about.

She shivered, huddling herself in her jacket. With bated breath, she watched as Peter's rock-like cocoon sat there for almost two hours, vibrating and making strange guttural noises.

Some time later, a loud cracking noise woke Mandy. She hadn't even realised she'd fallen asleep. She watched on, mouth agape as the mound began to crumble and fall away in parts. The mound swelled, revealing a transparent viscous layer.

She could see Peter inside, struggling against the strong glutinous shield that encased him. He was no longer in any pain. He felt calm as he was suspended motionless within his womb-like cocoon, surrounded by a layer of enriching vitamins, his cells regenerating.

But now it was time to be reborn.

He flailed his arms out, fighting against the thick shell until it began to break away. The dead flesh crumbled away in dark chunks that resembled charred wood. The contrasting viscosity underneath was smooth and placenta-like. It broke away from his face. He pushed his mouth through for air, gasping as he took a sharp intake of breath. He pushed his fingers through, liquid spilling forth, through and over the crumbling cocoon.

Peter did indeed resemble the Phoenix as the dead tissue matter dropped away from him in huge clumps and his fresh new body pushed through, being reborn from the ashes of his old body.

He fell in a heap onto the hard cave floor. The dismantled mound of new and decayed matter scattered around him. He lay there feeling vulnerable, naked, and shivering, covered in a sticky visceral ooze. Some particles of decay still stuck to the sticky surface of his body.

"Peter!" Mandy exclaimed, having watched the whole process in a manner of disturbed curiosity.

"Mandy," he croaked.

"Peter, are you okay? Peter?" she fussed about him, taking her coat off and placing it over his shivering frame.

"Mandy," he whispered weakly, awkwardly straining his neck to look up at her. "Oh, my god, Mandy. There are so many things I want to say to you, to explain and to thank you."

She shook her head, wanting him to save his energy. "Now is not the time. Are you okay to walk?"

"I'm not sure." It was a struggle, but after a few minutes he finally pushed himself up onto his weak legs.

"Good. Let's get you out of here before it's light enough for people to see you." She placed one hand around his waist and threw his arm over her shoulder, navigating him towards the cave entrance. It was difficult to get through the forest. The weight of his body was a strain upon her side, but she was determined to get him home safely.

Luckily the injured cop had been collected and taken to hospital without the caves being investigated. Apart from the sharp branches ripping at their sides, they managed to get back through the woods in less than an hour.

Mandy helped Peter into his house and into a warm bath. He was drained of energy as she washed him, dressed him and put him to bed. Mandy too felt exhausted, falling asleep in the chair that she had pulled up next to his bed. Peter had awoken in the night and had seen Mandy at his side. He smiled weakly, gratefully, and held her hand.

* * *

Peter took a large gulp of orange juice as he sat down at the kitchen table. He opened the morning newspaper. "Exclusive: Local cop shares his terrifying story of being attacked by a humanoid tree monster in the woods," he read aloud.

Mandy scoffed loudly, spooning scrambled eggs onto four pieces of buttered toast. "They're still going on about that?"

"Yeah, well, of course. It would have freaked anyone out!"

"Anyway, I'm deadlier than any so-called tree monster," she chuckled, placing their breakfast down on the kitchen table. She sat down opposite him, eyes fixed eagerly on her breakfast. "Eat up, you need to regain your energy."

"Thanks, honey," he said, swallowing a mouthful of egg. He nearly spluttered as he looked at the paper again. "Witness Sarah Summers also recounts her encounter with the monster. 'I know for certain that it was the fabled Phoenixis, as I have written about on my blog: Portland's Local Folklore'..." Peter groaned, pushing the paper away from him.

Instead, he smiled ferociously as he watched Mandy shovel the eggs into her mouth and chew frantically. "Did I ever tell you how much I appreciate you staying with me the night of my transformation?"

"Only every day!" she glared but then laughed.

"I mean it, Mand." He placed his hand on hers and squeezed it affectionately. "I probably would've been dead if you hadn't have saved me from the cop's bullets. Or worse, locked up in some laboratory to have my condition tested like a world-class freak."

"I have to admit, I was scared out of my mind when I first saw you in transition."

"I know, and yet you still stayed with me until you knew I was okay. Not many people would do that for each other. Even in the face of my horrendous condition, you understood and have accepted me for who I am."

"Well, shucks," she blushed, gripping his hand tightly. "We're going to have to make some sort of special room in the house for your transformation. Soundproof it or something. I'll be there for you when it happens."

They both leaned in for a kiss. Their lips parted

and Peter stared lovingly into her eyes. "I hope that means you'll move in with me?" Peter raised his eyebrows.

"Yeah, sure," she grinned. "Not like I've been waiting for you to ask..."

THE OVERWRITE

Linda's loud snoring woke Gary. With some effort, he lifted his sleepy head up from his desk. Light was just beginning to filter through the window, bathing their bedroom in a warm yellow glow. He looked around to see his wife Linda fast asleep in bed. He hadn't even realised that he'd fallen asleep at the desk again. He smacked his dry lips together, desperate for a morning coffee.

"Ergh," he grimaced, seeing the drool on his physics textbook. He wiped the pages dry with his sleeve, cursing at himself under his breath. He didn't want the university to fine him for accidentally damaging one of their books.

His mind was still racing at the concepts he'd been reading. Studying Mathematics and Applied Physics at his local university had melted his brain. His current quantum physics module had sent his imagination into overdrive. This was his first year and he wanted to ace his exams. He wouldn't admit to anyone that he found some of the concepts quite difficult to grasp. It wasn't so much the visualisation of them, it was the hard science part he struggled with. But to understand one, you had to understand the other. It was his dream to get a job as an engineer at

CERN, but he doubted he was smart enough to ever work there. The fact he had only just scraped through the entrance exam to get onto his university course always reminded him of this.

At the age of forty-two, he was a mature student. He had always considered himself an intelligent guy, but he was constantly being outdone by the annoying, genius twenty-somethings in his class, and it was severely denting his confidence.

There was this Korean kid, Min-jun, barely twenty, who had graduated high-school three years early because of his super genius IQ, could speak seven languages, and was an ice hockey champion. He seemed to be good at everything. Min-jun constantly outshone everyone in debates and always scored 100% on his tests. What's worse, he revealed that he opted to study the quantum physics module for fun to accompany his main studies in Astrophysics. For fun! Meanwhile, Gary was struggling. Min-jun had embarrassed Gary in his last lecture, reeling off a stream of in-depth facts about the Danish physicist Niels Bohr of whom he only knew the basics.

Gary had joked, "Don't be such a Bohr."

It hadn't gone down well.

Gary had then tried to look clever by talking about "interconnected particles." Min-jun proceeded to tell him, in front of everyone, that the correct phrase was *quantally entangled* particles, relating to the word quantum. He asked him how he could possibly not know that.

How could he live that down? Made him look like a fool, a red-faced, stupid buffoon. And to make matters even worse, Min-jun was so damn good-looking. Looked like a damn model as well as a genius. Gary knew it was immature, but he had taken an instant dislike to him. It was jealousy, but he would never dare admit it. He had googled the name Min-jun. Apparently Min meant "quick, clever and sharp" and Jun meant "talented and handsome." Min-jun was certainly living up to his name.

"Damn him." Gary ran a hand through his short, messy hair. Since that incident, he'd rarely left his desk, doing his best to cram in as such information as possible. But it was tiring. Exhaustion had consumed him. He sat at his desk, staring blankly around the room, thinking that he should get changed out of his pyjama top and shorts. But his mind soon turned back to his studies. There was no way he was going to pass his next test if he didn't knuckle down and study.

Gary felt that what he lacked in test scores, he made up for in imagination. He'd always had an over-active imagination. Gary particularly loved the concept of matter being in a duality, in both particle and wave form, and the notion that the observer can effect change onto physical reality. This opened up a myriad of theoretical possibilities to his mind. What if the observer could change their reality? Even though the observer would be a participant in that reality.

The multiverse was another concept he loved to visualise and ruminate on, that there were infinite parallel worlds existing alongside each other, lying just beyond this world. He imagined those worlds as infinite layers of information encoded onto the aether, information fluctuating between them, but they were just out of reach to our perception.

Linda continued to snore loudly.

His wife Linda often said that she was concerned for him, his mind being away with the fairies, that being deeply troubled by these wild quantum theories was irrational. Gary had agreed and thought the best thing he could do was do some normal things for a while — go see a football game, a film, go food shopping, wash the car, etc. Some normal, banal activities to bring his wild imagination back down to earth.

But he couldn't stop thinking about quantum theories. He had to pass his exams. His pride was at stake.

Gary stared over at Linda. Her foot was peeking out of the covers and she lay in an awkward position that looked really uncomfortable. He smiled to himself. He thought that Linda was the best thing to have ever happened to him. They had been married for five years, and had been dating for another seven years before that. In their twelve years together, she had always kept him grounded.

"Linda!" he shouted, trying to cut through her snoring. That was one thing he didn't like about her, but he knew that she couldn't help it. Gary stretched his arms out into the air and yawned. Still feeling reflective, he stared up at a framed photo of his parents, Susan and David. His father was a skinny bald man and his mother was a large woman with grey hair cut into a bob. They'd always been great parents, so loving and caring.

It had been strange moving back into his parent's house, the place he grew up as a child. His parents had wanted a smaller place, and Gary and Linda had wanted to move out of their pokey flat and into a bigger place, so it seemed like a fair swap.

Linda continued to snore. He joked that once she was asleep, she was the "unwakeable object", and no amount of shouting would rouse her from her slumber.

But tickling would.

"Linda! Oh, Linda!" He decided to wake her up. He hurried over to her, throwing himself onto the bed, finding the shape of a body beneath the mass of quilts. He threw the quilt over his head and started to tickle her sides.

"Lindaaaa!"

"Get off!" she shrieked, half asleep, annoyed at being woken up, but laughing at the tickling. She hit out at him, hitting him square in the stomach.

"Ow!" he roared before they settled down to hugging each other in bed.

"Where were you? Asleep at the desk again?"

"Yeah, sorry. I was reading about quantum theory again, trying to get my head around the more scientific studies of its principles."

"Oh, yeah... What you been reading this time?"

she said groggily, rubbing her tired eyes.

"Well, apart from my textbooks, I've been reading The Holographic Universe. I love the idea that reality could be perceptible to change, that changes could enfold from the aether and materialise into concrete reality. I wondered if we would even be aware of it if it did?" He stared out into space, looking troubled.

He'd gone down the intellectual rabbit hole many times, wavering from scientific principle to pseudoscience to conspiracy theories, and everything in between. He was open-minded to all concepts.

"Hmm, okay. I'll pretend to know what you're on about," Linda sniffed, trying to settle back into the comfortable quilt.

"My latest obsession is reading online about reality changes. A large number of people around the world believe that reality has changed because they remember things like celebrities dying who are suddenly alive again, countries moving location, different major world events, etc." He laughed it off, probably a faulty mass memory, although then what would cause that to happen? It did intrigue him, both scientifically and theoretically.

"They're just nutters!" Linda glared at him.

"There could be some validation to it. It is just a theory after all."

"You're crazy."

"Oh, thanks." Gary took the huff, staring squarely at his disgruntled wife.

"You are because you actually believe in those crazy theories about parallel universes and reality changes. It's all bullshit. People just remember stuff wrong. Why do you like to believe in those crackpot theories? Do you think it makes you look clever or something? Can't you just appreciate what is right here in front of you?" She screwed up her face.

He felt hurt. Linda making fun of his studies, as if it was a waste of time and energy, really upset him. It was bad enough that he already doubted himself, and that Min-jun constantly overshadowed him, let alone the love of his life doubting him. His head began to swim with anxiety. His eyes started to feel heavy and his vision started to become blurry.

"Why are you being like this? You know I love you more than anything."

"I'm always here, right in front of you, but you'd rather be hunched over your desk all night reading books instead," she said angry and hastily, as if she'd been bottling this up for a long time. It was finally exploding from her mouth with full impact.

"That's not fair. You always said you'd support me in my studies. Once I graduate this course, I want to do a master's degree in quantum physics."

"I did say I'd support you, but lately you've become obsessed with all this nonsense. It's all you ever think about. It's consumed you. You're taking it too far. You might as well disappear into another universe."

"That's harsh!" Gary winced, a sharp pain

suddenly cut through his head and his vision was becoming increasingly blurry and distorted.

"I could understand it if you wanted to do something useful, like become a surgeon. But a quantum physics degree? What you gonna do with that?"

"I could become a science teacher." He was desperately trying to concentrate on Linda's face, but she was fading out of view. His eyes started to water and a ringing noise pierced his ears, making it difficult to concentrate. The ringing noise subdued, turning into a low hum.

"But then you'll have to do a teaching degree as well. University costs too much. We can't afford it. I'm already working two jobs to help you indulge your fantasies, and pay the bills, let alone save for anything exciting. I have ambitions and dreams of my own, you know." There was bitterness in her voice. "I want to travel to America and East Asia. We haven't been on an exciting holiday in years. I'm so bored with life."

Gary thought about all those handsome Asian geniuses like Min-jun, and shuddered. "Hell no. You don't need to go East Asia."

"I don't *need* to. I *want* to," she shot back.

"Anyway, I said I'd pay you back. Once I get a decent job, I'll pay you and mum back and we'll be fine," he said woozily, caressing his forehead with his fingers, wondering why his head felt so weird. He blinked rapidly, but the air around him looked like it was throbbing and vibrating.

"You haven't had a decent job for years. It's all fantasy, just like your studies." She took his hand and put it to her chest. "See, I'm real, unlike your silly theories!"

"I can feel you, but my head feels weird. I can barely see you." Gary began to panic.

"Probably freaking yourself out again with those outlandish stories from freaks on the internet. You could be cuddling me instead, but no..." She turned away.

He blinked rapidly, struggling to keep his eyes open against the pain in his head. Linda's body looked faint, as if she was disappearing. All of a sudden, she was gone.

Gary did a double-take, unable to move, trying to fathom what was happening. "Seriously, Linda, I can't see you!" he cried.

"I might as well be invisible to you then," she said coldly.

Gary jumped. "What's happening? I can hear you, but I can't see you." He felt around the bed. He could feel her body, but the bed before him appeared empty.

"Get off me!" she shrugged him off. He felt his hands being pushed away. He could feel something he could no longer see.

A deep fear came over him. "Linda. I'm being serious. I think there's something wrong with me. I can't see you!"

"I'm sorry," he heard her say. He was terrified, wondering if he was having a seizure or if he had a brain tumour, or something that could account for this.

Gary attempted to get out of bed, but Linda pulled him back down onto the bed. He felt restrained by an invisible force.

"What the hell?" he shrieked.

"What's wrong with you?" Linda's voiced asked, sounding like a spectral voice on the wind. "Look, I'm sorry for being so horrible. I didn't mean to be so mean. I just feel like we've become distant lately. I don't want this crap to come between us. Just kiss me, god damn it!" she asked. Invisible hands pulled him closer.

Gary felt bewildered as he felt himself being pulled through the air. He felt her lips land on his cheek. There was nobody visibly there, yet there was the feeling of solidarity and a palpable touch on his skin. It was as if she was a ghost.

Could it be...? Gary thought suddenly. Could Linda have disappeared into another reality somehow metaphysically entwined with this one? Or was it he who was disappearing? Were they between the aether of two dimensions pressed against each other? Was he the participant who had become the observer of reality change? The thought horrified him.

"LINDA! Don't disappear!" he cried, throwing his arms around her, as if trying to solidify her, to pull her back into this world, or for him to somehow get back into that world.

"Gary? What is it?" he suddenly heard his mother's voice calling out to him.

Gary went deadly still, feeling startled. A feeling of deep dread pulsated through him. "Mum?" he replied quietly, his heart racing, fearing he had imagined her voice. He was wondering if he had gone insane.

The door opened.

"What's wrong, love? Have you had another nightmare?" his mum asked, obviously concerned as to why he was calling out so urgently.

"What are you doing here?" he roared, sheepishly pulling the covers over him, bemused as he regarded her appearance. She looked different to usual. Her hair was a lot longer. It had been straightened and highlighted with blonde streaks. She was wearing large round glasses and looked a lot slimmer than usual. This was all very out of character for her, and he was taken aback to how her appearance could have changed so drastically overnight.

"What do you mean what am I doing here? I live here!" She screwed up her face, a mixture of concern and annoyance in her expression.

"You moved out..."

She didn't answer, looking exasperated.

Deep down, deep within his gut, Gary's instinct told him that he had travelled into an alternate dimension or that reality had changed. His rational mind was doing its best to come up with a conclusion, no matter how illogical, to retain a sense of normality, a coping mechanism so he didn't go into meltdown.

"Why do you look so different?" Gary asked.

"I don't look any different to usual," she pulled a disgruntled face. Again, something his incredibly warm and kind mother would never do.

Gary narrowed his eyes suspiciously, but kept schtum. Movement in the corner of his eye caught his attention. He glanced at the mirror on the side table. He could see Linda within it. "Oh my god, Linda! I can see you in the mirror!" he exclaimed, but he still couldn't see her on the bed.

"Who are you talking to? Your mum isn't here. I told you you've gone crazy!" Linda shouted, looking worried.

"Who are you talking to?" his mum asked, peering around at the empty bed.

Gary felt flummoxed. "Look at this…" He picked up the mirror and held it up towards his face. He moved it around and Linda's actions eerily corresponded within the reflection.

"Look at what?" his mum asked, walking around to the other side of the bed to peer into it.

"Look in the mirror!"

She bent down slightly and squinted, and then looked at him like he'd gone insane. "I can see your face in the mirror," she said.

"Look, there's Linda in the mirror. Yet she's not physically here!"

"I can only see you."

"Y-you can't see her?" he stammered. The colour

drained from his face. Sweat trickled down the nape of his neck.

The Linda in the mirror was staring at him. "Why are you talking to yourself?" Linda asked. When Gary heard her speak, it was like hearing a voice in the back of his mind. Like when you think you hear a voice but you haven't, like an auditory hallucination.

"No. I see you waving a mirror around talking like a crazy person, though. This is the psychological effects of your divorce. Part of your mental breakdown, but we can get you help," she said bluntly.

"We... what? Mental breakdown? We would never get divorced!" Gary whimpered.

"Yes, you did. You got divorced. It's about time that you accept it so you can recover some sanity," she remarked scathingly.

"Sure, I sometimes annoy and bore Linda with my babbling about quantum theories, but we always make up after arguments. That's what couples do."

"Your quantum what?"

"My quantum theories studies at university! You and Linda helped me financially so I could become a teacher!"

"Oh, please, Gary. You'll always be a builder. You love to graft. It's in your blood. You could never do a job like teaching. All the paperwork teachers have to do! You'd be so bored by all that pen-pushing! I'm sorry that you have invented this fantasy world in an attempt to cover your grief."

"What? I'm not living in a fantasy world! I've

never built a thing in my life! I can barely put up shelves. Isn't that right, Linda? Linda! Where are you?" Gary trailed off, glaring into the mirror. Linda had disappeared from the mirror. Gary panicked, feeling around the bed. He couldn't even feel her invisible body anymore.

"Oh, Linda. Where have you gone? I hope I haven't lost you forever!" he cried, scrunching up the bedsheets in his hands, sobbing hysterically.

His mum stared at him in silent horror.

"Maybe I've travelled into another dimension so that's why I have the ability to see what's beyond. I'm an observer. I can see what's happening in the other world because I was once there. Some sort of freaky metaphysical insight into worlds that lie parallel to our own," he indicated with his hands, staring wildly at his perplexed mum. The alternative that he was suffering a mental breakdown with delusions seemed just as terrifying a prospect as having moved through dimensions and that reality had suddenly changed around him.

His mum continued to stare at him like he'd gone completely mad. "Mm, hmm," she said, before lingering near the bedroom door. "Dave, come here!" she yelled.

Gary was surprised. His mum never calls his dad Dave. She always calls him David.

"Yes, Karen?" his dad replied meekly, walking up to the doorway.

"Karen? Your name is Susan!" Gary shouted.

"Susan?" she frowned. "Okay, I'm really worried about you now."

Gary was flabbergasted at what his father looked like, too. Nothing like his usual self. He now had shoulder-length, wavy, grey hair and was dressed in distressed blue jeans, a white shirt and a multi-coloured waistcoat that resembled a kitchen rug.

"You look like a freaking hippy!" Gary cried.

"I think we need to take Gary back to the doctor," she whispered. "He's getting a bit hysterical and having hallucinations of Linda. Perhaps we should have had him admitted to the mental hospital after all." She didn't whisper quietly enough.

"I don't need to go to a doctor! A mental hospital? No!" Gary cried.

"You sort this out, Dave. I need to get back to my pottery studio," she said dismissively.

"Pottery? What the fuck? You don't have a creative bone in your body!"

"Charming," she snorted, looking offended. She walked away and headed down the stairs.

"Please, watch your language," Dave said, without any conviction in his voice. He was usually an argumentative, fiery character, so Gary found it bizarre that he was being so meek and mild. He found his "opposite" parents totally confusing. This dad was pathetically mousy and this mum was an irritating, stone cold, uncaring bitch — completely unlike their usual characters. These alternate parents seemed so strict and uncaring, even in the midst of his so-called mental breakdown. Gary missed his real, loving parents.

"What's going on? I'm worried about you. You're not handling the break up well, which is understandable after you've been together for so long," Dave said calmly, sitting down on the bed next to him.

"Don't give me this bullshit advice like some internet horoscope guru dishing out generic rubbish!" Gary protested.

Dave remained silent.

"Look," Gary said, getting annoyed. "Woah," he said, suddenly feeling light-headed again. An intense pain shot through his scalp and the ringing noise in his ears returned for a few seconds. It felt like someone had taken a hammer to his head. His vision went all wavy and the room seemed to glitch and flash, like some sort of material status had solidified. He noticed that in the corner of the room, where his desk had been, there was now suddenly a wardrobe there.

"Where the hell did that wardrobe come from?" Gary cried, shaking now because it was obvious that reality was solidifying more into this freaky parallel world. He could feel the change in the air. It had become denser and less woozy.

"Wardrobe?" Dave took off his round glasses to clean them.

"That bloody wardrobe over there!" Gary pointed towards it, waving his finger up and down for extra effect.

Dave sighed. "That wardrobe has always been there," he answered matter-of-factly.

"There was a desk there, just a few moments ago! It had a computer on it and loads of my science books. God damn it!"

"Please calm down. I want to understand what you're going through. I want to try to help you." Dave rubbed his glasses with a cloth and put them back on his thin nose.

"No, I won't calm down. I think I have the right to get flustered. I'm trapped in a world and life that isn't my own and there's nothing I can do about it. Furthermore, I'm the only person aware of the transition."

Dave raised his eyebrows questioningly.

Gary looked at the lamp behind the mirror on the bedside table. The lampshade had morphed from a grey material to a purple one. He grabbed the mirror and stared into it. It was just a normal mirror now.

"The connection to my world has been severed, lost. It infuriates me to think of everything and everyone I've left behind. Even though this reality is similar, it couldn't feel more abnormal and alien than it does right now. Is this what happens in normal everyday life? Reality alters and we are oblivious to it? It's a terrifying thought. My awareness has somehow escaped the overwrite. No wonder I feel like I'm going mad. Surely this would drive anyone to the edge, being a blip, being the only spectator in the true fluctuating nature of reality. What if I can't go back?" Gary babbled on, his eyes wide with terror.

"What the hell are you talking about? Reality hasn't changed." Dave looked horrified, seeing his son gibbering away like a madman.

Gary wrapped the quilt tightly around him, pale, shaking and sweating.

"Okay, please listen, Dad. What I'm about to tell you may sound unbelievable, but please believe me. I'm not your Gary. I've somehow filtered through from a parallel timeline or dimension that is very similar to this one. Layered against each other, like this," he said, positioning his hands upright in a prayer motion.

"Your world..." he moved one hand away. "And my world..." he did the same with the other, "became quantally entangled. *Quantally*. I know that because of Min-jun."

"Who the hell is Min-jun?"

Gary ignored him and continued to explain. "But some sort of cosmic catalyst effected a change. The two worlds collided and your world overtook mine. My reality got overwritten and I somehow got trapped here. Well, that's how I imagine it anyway. I escaped the overwrite." He clasped his hands together in a lame demonstration of quantum movement.

Dave looked at him like he was mad.

"Do you understand?" Gary asked nervously.

Dave sighed, readjusting his glasses and puffing out his cheeks. "I understand. I just worry why you believe this is happening." He folded his arms and studied him.

Gary felt enraged. "What? This *is* happening! I'm not having a mental breakdown, am I? Oh, my god, am I having a breakdown? Am I crazy?" He rocked back and forth on the bed, eyes bulging with terror.

Dave placed his arm around Gary in an attempt to be comforting, but his touch was rigid and devoid of any love. Gary flinched. He guessed that the version of himself here wasn't close with his parents like he was back in his world. He felt an extreme emptiness inside.

"You're having an emotional meltdown because of your breakup with Linda. I can help you. I'll call Doctor Bletchem. Your therapy sessions went well with her. We can make you better."

Gary didn't have a clue who Doctor Bletchem was. He stared into the distance, burying his chin into the soft quilt. His eyes welled up with tears. He let them fog over with misery.

"Okay," Gary whispered. It made sense that his parents would think he was insane from his crazy talk. But he was scared that his father would convince him that he was actually insane, and that his previous life that had been cruelly ripped away from him was just a delusion. He couldn't accept that. He knew he wasn't crazy.

Was he?

No… he had to somehow hang on to the truth. But that was going to be difficult to play along at acting normal, to get used to life here.

What was life like here? He didn't know anything about this world. Even the slightest of differences threw everything off, culminating in an alternative world. Variant choices had made life so different, made people so vastly different, made everything different — names, details, emotions, aesthetics, objects. And then further differences in social constructs — different talents, different jobs and different relationships. The list was endless. The possibilities were endless.

Gary started to question his sanity. Surely crazy people didn't realise they were crazy? Therefore, by definition, he couldn't be crazy. Or did that mean he was crazy? He felt too overwhelmed to think properly.

"Gary..." his dad said tenderly.

But Gary continued to think. Maybe his mind had invented this quantum shift as a hallucination when his relationship broke down. But he didn't remember his marriage breaking down because only half an hour ago he'd been in his own world with the love of his life, Linda. She was so angry with him for favouring his studies over her. How could this quantum shift be true? He wished he'd never got obsessed with it. He wished he'd just concentrated on his own life and been oblivious to all this. He wished he'd never gone down the quantum rabbit hole and questioned the nature of existence. He was just a mere mortal. He'd do anything to go back to being ignorant, oblivious and unaware. This is what he'd wanted for so long, to be enlightened to the true nature of reality. His metaphorical questions had been answered. But being enlightened was no fun. It was torture. This was hell.

Gary started to sob hysterically. "I want to go home!"

"You are home," his dad said sadly.

The room begin to throb as if deep energy fluctuations were rippling through its matter. Gary got up from the bed. He stood there agape and dumbstruck, watching as the structure of the room began to morph before his eyes. Walls began to crackle and change, moving closer or further back. He could see several faint layers of reality overlapping and combining. The wooden window frames descended down and through the wall, and solidified into a smaller window. Small square panes of glass filled the slats, replacing the larger panes.

"Did you just see that?" Gary whimpered.

"Did I see what?" Dave asked. He was now wearing a blue shirt and his hair was now short and auburn.

"Your hair! It's red now. You've always been bald. It was long and grey a moment ago!" Gary shrieked, pulling his fingernails down his face.

"Gary, I've always had red hair." His father shook his head, looking pained at Gary's confusion.

"This is more than just two worlds colliding. I'm moving through continual changes. I am moving through the multiverse. The barrier between the many worlds pressed together has somehow broken down.

Or at least my barrier of perception has!" Gary cried, still trying to explain it to himself.

"Gary, please…"

"What the fuck is happening? I'm going mad. I've gone mad!" Gary ran over to the window. He watched on in horror as the wardrobe turned into a chest of drawers and green leather armchairs appeared upon polished floorboards which now had replaced the carpet. Gary peered through the now small window with watering eyes to see a picturesque cul-de-sac instead of his usual urban street. Beautiful blossom trees now stood between the streetlights. The air felt different again. It was a different place. A different world. Any sense of familiarity had been stripped away from him. He'd always taken the comfort of familiarity for granted.

"What is this? Where am I now? What's happening?" Gary cried, collapsing to the floor. He stared around him. The process seemed to speed up. His father's visage continued to change. His clothes morphed into different ones, his eyes changed colour from green to blue to brown, his hair changed colour and length, and different accessories appeared upon him.

The wall colours changed, the room got smaller, bigger, the furniture morphed into different objects or new furniture appeared from nowhere or simply disappeared. The accompanying audio was horrible; a cacophony of discordant overlapping sounds — voices and sounds of appliances and outside activity throbbing in and out of existence.

Gary screamed, putting his hands over his head, not wanting to see or hear any changes. He couldn't handle this torture. He stayed there as reality continued to change around him at an alarming speed.

Everything changed again.

And again.

And again.

And again.

And again.

And again.

THE PRINCE'S TAVERN

Dark, heavy clouds rolled ominously across the evening sky. Lizzie had barely got her umbrella up over her head before the rain was battering down on it. Raindrops pitter-pattered on its acrylic surface as she ran towards the bus stop. It was the last bus home and it waited patiently next to the flagpole.

The wind turned her umbrella inside out. She groaned, trying to pull it back down as she ran, but the metal rods had all bent out of shape.

"No! Please wait!" she groaned as the bus's back indicator flashed to pull out. Her side hurt as she bolted in a last attempt to flag the driver down. But it was hopeless as the bus continued onwards. She stopped and stared dejectedly as the bus turned the corner and drove out of sight.

"Damn it! If only I'd been a few seconds earlier," she huffed, sitting down on a wall opposite the bus stop, getting totally drenched, mangled umbrella in her lap. Her grey, two-piece work suit had soaked through, clinging to her skin. Her wet, mousy-brown hair hung limply around her face.

She sighed, reaching into her handbag for her mobile phone. She chose the most-dialled number from the call list. "Hey, babe. I've missed the last bloody home… Yes, I know… My boss kept me late to discuss the job transfer to Sweden. What? No! Look, I didn't plan for this to happen. It's not like I enjoy being stranded. No, it's too far, a taxi would cost too much. I'll stay in a hotel for the night. Yeah. Bye. I love…"

There was a sudden beeping noise. She looked at her phone. Paul had hung up on her.

"You." She rolled her eyes. Her relationship with her long-time beau, Paul, had been rocky for quite some time now. Ever since she'd announced that she'd been offered a job in Stockholm, and she was considering taking it, Paul had told her to stay in London, and from then on refused to discuss the situation. It infuriated her as she wanted to be able to make plans, and if it came to it, with or without him. He had been sleeping in the spare room for the last couple of weeks. She loved him more than anything, but they were both incredibly stubborn and unable to compromise.

Perhaps being stranded was a good thing. Perhaps she needed a night on her own anyway, to relax and collect her thoughts.

She pulled up an app on her phone to see what cheap accommodation was available for the night. There were a few places nearby.

"The Grand Hotel De Luxe. £75 a night… Nope. Davey's Bed and Breakfast. Two stars and bad reviews… Nope."

She stopped suddenly, her thumb hovering over a

bed and breakfast, a small inn called 'The Prince's Tavern'. Feeling drawn to the place for some inexplicable reason, she looked on the tariff page. It was only £34 for the night. She glared at the picture. A strange feeling came over her. She felt like she must stay there. Pulling up a map on her phone, she headed for Doncaster Road. It was a ten-minute walk or so, but for some odd reason she felt compelled that it was worth the effort.

The Prince's Tavern was located in the historic quarter of the city. Rightly so, it had refused to be brought into the modern age. Its old-fashioned, grand buildings remained largely untouched from the Victorian era. She had never been around this part of town before. Its Gothic buildings were alluringly creepy. Their gloomy presence was part of their architectural beauty.

Just one more corner, she thought. She wrinkled her nose, confused as to why she already seemed to know the way.

She saw the sign before she'd even got there. The tavern's signage board was stuck up on the wall of the old, rickety-looking building. The image of a prince sat under the calligraphic lettering which read, 'The Prince's Tavern'. Deep blue eyes stared back at her. Overwhelmed by the biggest sense of déjà vu, she stared up at the tavern's front and swallowed hard. She felt inexplicably strange and uncomfortable. The prince was a handsome man, with blond hair and striking features.

"Get a grip," she told herself. Shaking off the uncomfortable vibe, she entered the tavern entrance and walked up to the bar. There were a few locals drinking in the corner, and a few of people at the other end, sitting around a table. One man sat on a barstool, draining the last of his ale. He had long, wispy, grey hair and wore a leather jacket, jeans and boots. An old biker sort.

"Another one please, Mike," he said in a thick Scottish accent.

"Raining outside, is it?" the man behind the bar said. A stocky, bearded man with a kind face. Mike, she guessed. He pushed a pint glass underneath the beer tap and pulled the lever.

Lizzie smiled, knowing she was drenched. "Just a bit," she chortled, trying to push back her wet brown hair that was stuck to her face.

"How can I help you, m'dear?" he asked, placing the newly filled pint in front of the Scottish man. He took the change and entered it into the till.

"I wondered if you have any rooms available? I missed the last bus home from work and I need somewhere to stay, only for one night."

"Sounds like you're in a bit of a pickle. Sure, we have some rooms available. Business is slow this time of year. My name's Mike." He extended his hand towards her.

"Lizzie." She shook his hand and smiled. "I shouldn't think you have that many rooms in such a small building, do you?"

"I suppose not," he smirked. "But those four bedrooms are often in demand," he winked amusingly.

"I bet," she laughed. "Although in the early 1800s there used to be six bedrooms until there was a fire next door which nearly burnt down half of the tavern, so one side had to be rebuilt..." She suddenly realised what she was saying and fell quiet in bemusement, wondering where this information was coming from.

Mike padded over to a shelf, glancing at her wearily, and took a ring of metal keys from a nail on the wall. The keys rattled as he pushed the other keys around the ring. "Yup. Not many people know that. You a local history buff?"

"Kinda," she made an excuse. She couldn't fathom how she innately knew these details. Luckily, Mike took over the conversation.

"£34 for the night. I accept cash or credit card. We're not totally stuck in the past!" His pleasant sense of humour put her at ease.

"Brilliant. Thank you. I'll pay by card," she said, pushing her card into the chip and pin machine, then entered her pin number for the payment to be processed.

"Full name and contact details, please," he asked, getting out a book and pen.

"Elizabeth Hartwell. 75 Sugden Drive, London." She got the details out of the way and smiled as the payment went through.

"This way," he said, opening the wooden panel of the bar doorway. He pushed a wooden door open to reveal some stone steps. Lizzie followed him up the narrow stairs until they got to the landing.

"I'll put you in the room overlooking the street. It's the cosiest room. Although some folk call it the haunted chamber." The smile fell from his face slightly, but he covered it up with a laugh.

"Haunted?"

"I don't believe in all that myself. Never seen or heard anything while I've owned the place, but a lot of guests say they can hear voices come from the walls; Swedish accents in particular. I think they just read into the hype of the prince who stayed here in the 1800s. The place is dedicated to him, hence why it's named The Prince's Tavern."

"Prinsens värdshus," Lizzie mumbled in Swedish. The words stunned her. She didn't even know any Swedish, or so she thought.

Mike stared at her for a moment, a quizzical look on his face. "Yeah, how did you know?"

"Maybe I am a bit of a history buff," she lied, smiling weakly.

Mike grinned. "Well, the tavern is steeped in rich foreign history. It's the unusual back stories that have earned us so many customers. That and our great lemon meringue," he chuckled.

Lizzie stared into space, feeling bewildered.

Mike coughed to break the sudden awkward silence. "Well, it's nice when folk take an interest in local businesses and their history." He took a key and opened the door to a room on the left of the hallway.

"I hope you enjoy your stay. If you need anything just ring the extension on line one which will put you through to the phone in my room or the phone in reception."

"Thank you very much," Lizzie nodded.

"Or if you're that desperate then just knock on my door, which is just down there and around the corner. The bar closes in half an hour so it should be quiet from then on, unless you hear voices or anything..."

"I certainly hope not," she replied, walking into the centre of the room. She placed her handbag down onto the bed.

"Breakfast is served between eight and ten in the morning. Check-out time is between eleven and twelve."

"Oh, I forgot to say. I'll be checking out around eight anyway, as I have to be at work for nine."

"Sure, just leave your key at the bar in the morning with me, my wife Janice, or one of the other staff. Like I said, if you need any refreshments or food, Jan and I will be around so just give us a shout and we'll bring it up to you."

"Thank you."

"Freshly pressed towels and dressing gowns are in the wardrobe," he said as he glanced at her sodden work suit.

"You cater to my every need!" As nice as he was, she wanted him to leave so she could settle down.

His greying moustache twitched as he beamed, hoping for a five-star review online, no doubt. "Good night then," he said, closing the door behind him.

"Night," she said, locking the door behind her. Finally. Some peace and quiet.

She kicked off her shoes and headed straight for the bathroom. She took off her clothes and laid them out on the radiators. Hopefully they would be dry by morning. She headed straight for the shower, feeling the welcome warmth of the hot water stream down onto her aching body and the comforting aroma of the shower gel. The deep, invigorating smell of verbena wafted up her nose she lathered up, making the whole room smell fragrant.

Once she'd finished showering, she dried off, opening the windows to let the steam out and then retreated to the bedroom. She flopped down on the bed and turned towards the tea and biscuits laid out on the side table. As she waited for the kettle to boil, she popped a tiny complimentary shortbread in her mouth and chewed frantically, considering ordering something to eat. She then made some tea and sat back to sip it, placing it on the side table. She felt her heavy eyelids come crashing down. The radiating warmth of the dressing gown was making her feel sleepy.

As she descended into a light slumber, she thought about how strange this place was. How on earth was it possible that she knew the Swedish namesake of the tavern and knew details about a place she had never previously visited? It seemed so bizarre. She began to lose focus of her stream of thought as she began to fall asleep.

"Maria, kom hit, min älskling!"

The words crashed around Lizzie's head, causing her to jolt and flail around on the bed until she sat up, staring around the room in disbelief.

"Maria, come here my darling!" she translated out loud, breathing heavily, feeling scared stiff. The voices Mike had warned her about were real. She had distinctly heard a jovial male voice with a heavy Swedish accent. She swung her legs off the bed, but sat there motionless, not sure how to react.

"No, Master Havstam! My father might hear us."

"Varför retar du mig?"

"I do not tease you, Mikael!" a girlish reply bound around the room, resonance from a participant no longer visible.

Lizzie sat there breathing as shallowly as possible, straining to hear more voices abound from the silence.

It all felt so familiar, it felt so…

"How dare you turn down the advances from the prince of Sweden!" a male voice laughed. The voices sounded louder now, cutting through her bemused thoughts. The sounds of giggling and footsteps crashed around the room. It sounded like two people were amorously chasing each other.

There was a ruffle of underskirts swooshing through the air and the sound of leather boots being thrown against the wall. The audio of the scene was being played out, like an echo from the past. Lizzie's eyes darted around the room. She was frustrated that she couldn't see who was making the noise.

"Oooh," Lizzie breathed heavily, feeling a sudden wave of lust rush over her. She clenched the quilt tightly with both hands, rucking it up.

"You are the tease! Teasing me because you know I can never resist!" This time the voice was female with a broad London accent, young and bubbly.

"Tease me some more, my prince."

Lizzie pushed herself up from the bed and ran into the bathroom, panicking. She didn't feel right at all. She felt hot and bothered, sweating as she gripped the sink tightly, staring into the steamed up mirror. She wiped it over with the palm of her hand. Her head felt so heavy. It felt like the air was changing around her. As she stared at her reflection, she saw it morph before her eyes. She thought of the prince and the voices. If she was experiencing some revival of a past life, she had expected to see Maria's face before her. But instead, she saw messy blond hair, striking facial features and a ruffled white linen shirt.

She gasped, but didn't jump back, staring intently into the mirror. She turned her head to the left, seeing the prince's head move in the same direction. She admired his lean neck, looking down through his open shirt to see an athletic body. It was lean rather than muscled. The sweat on his collarbone made him sparkle with sensuality. His personality emanated from his adulterous smile.

He was wantonly handsome, but she didn't feel attracted to him. Moreover, she felt like she was him. She touched her face with her fingers and watched him touch his face, examining his porcelain skin and his angular face, mussing up his hair so it flopped down near to his deep blue eyes. He was vain, but not in an unpleasant sense. He knew how to promote his best features to benefit him.

Lizzie felt the sense of herself disappearing as she allowed the character of the prince to take over. He swaggered back into the bedroom. There was a young plump woman lying on the bed. She had such a lovely face, a warm and kind aura about her. Affection overwhelmed him. He loved her so much.

"My Maria," he said, pulling her into his arms, kissing her passionately on the lips.

"But I'm not just yours, am I? How many other girls have been invited to your bed of late?" Maria's voice stung with jealousy.

Mikael thought of the other women he invited to his bed, but Maria was the only one he actually loved. "None at all compare to you. While I am here, you are my Maria." He enclosed his arms around her tightly.

"I bet you have a girl in every city, in every country!"

"That's not your concern," Mikael said, turning her head to kiss her once more. Lizzie felt the lustful sensation returning. Lizzie had never been attracted to women, but she felt inexplicably aroused as she touched Maria's curvy body and kissed her, pushing her down onto the bed. Lizzie felt raw and attractive in her statuesque male body, full of swagger and testosterone.

"And I am one of the lucky ones who gets to have you?" Maria stared at him with questioning eyes.

Mikael nodded, grinning. He traced a finger over the scar on Maria's temple. An indentation from when she had accidentally fallen once in the kitchen and nearly skewered her head on a metal poker.

"Lower class girls have such characters, full of the hardships of life, heads not filled with grandeur."

Maria's affectionate tone suddenly changed at his comment, her mood becoming disconsolate. "My father once told me that most people harbour the secret desire for someone that they can't have. The fact that they can't have them, or shouldn't have them, is what makes the challenge so enticing and wanton. People want to taste the forbidden fruit of the passionate embrace," Maria told him as he stroked her hair and breathed in the aroma of lard and lavender on her hair from her kitchen duties.

Maria fingered a gold button that was stitched onto Mikael's splendid jacket. Her mind reeled at how much it must have cost, furthering her financial torment. "I think it might be true for some people, but there is also love, that one person will be good enough without lusting after others."

"But you can have me, Maria. I am yours forever," Mikael said earnestly. The words were coming from his mouth, in his melodic Swedish accent, yet Lizzie almost remembered saying every word, as if recalling a distant memory. She felt so naive back then as the prince, so young, so arrogant. Maria was a woman of the world, and even at the same age, she knew much more about life and people than he did.

Maria suddenly pushed him away, looking sorrowful. "You claim we are forever, but we are not! You come here to visit England occasionally while your father, the King of Sweden, God bless him, is on royal business in London, and you kiss me and make love to me and promise me nice things. And how I wish and imagine marrying you and bearing your children, but we both know these things can ever happen, no matter how much we want them to. I know I'm just a maid, but I'm not stupid. You'll return back home and court some other women, marry a beautiful Swedish princess, and live happily ever after. You'll forget about me."

"I could never forget you, Maria!" Mikael cried, feeling hurt.

But Maria continued on. "And I'll be stuck here for the rest of my boring life thinking on what ifs and maybes, getting even fatter and older with a husband I don't care for, having his children and forever thinking about you, forever loving you, and knowing these times are the best I'll ever get in my sorry life, and I don't expect this life from you, I don't expect anything from you, because I know it can never be." She turned away, tears stinging her eyes, staring out to the bleak smoggy view through the small window.

Mikael went quiet, sitting behind her, not knowing what to say.

"An' it breaks my heart because I keep getting a taste of this exciting life, and every time you leave I wonder if it's the last time I'll ever see you. It breaks my heart every time you arrive and every time you leave. It's worse than never having a taste at all. Sometimes the dreaming and hoping and never getting isn't as bad as having it and losing it. I just can't do this anymore, Mikael."

"Maria, I..." The pain was immense. He knew the end was coming. He could already feel his heart breaking. "I do love you, but the Swedish royal family is a life I was born into. I have no choice but to marry into royalty. I am third in line to the throne after my two elder brothers. I cannot deny my birth right."

"And I don't want you to." Maria's face was full of resentment and sorrow. Lizzie could feel Mikael's heartache as he saw how much pain he was causing her.

"Therein lies the problem, my love. Our lives can never be compatible. We will always be kept apart by our social backgrounds, and there's nothing we can do about it."

"But there is!" he said, grabbing her by the wrist as she attempted to leave the room. "I will continue to visit you in secret."

"I am sorry, Mikael. Your heart is good, but you do not see the truth." She stroked his face tenderly and kissed him on the lips, a long lingering kiss that made his lips tingle. "This is why I have agreed to marry another man. My father is trying to set me up with a local man, David McBride. He is kind at heart, doing well in business, and he feels it will be good for me. I am considering it." Her hazel eyes filled with wet sorrow as she stared into his deep blue eyes.

"No! I will not let you marry another man just for the sake of convenience!" Mikael roared.

"Sometimes convenience is the only life people like me can aspire to. Please, Mikael. It would be kinder if you never came here to see me ever again." Her voice broke as she tried not to break down and cry.

Mikael shook his head, not wanting to hear this.

"Please, if you if you love me as much as I love you, my darling, you will never return here."

"No, Maria!" he cried, trying to take her by the hand.

"I bid you farewell, my love." Tears rolled down Maria's cheeks as she took one last look at Mikael and then turned away. She pulled her voluminous dress back around her, smoothing the skirt out, and then left the room. She tried to compose herself as she walked down the narrow stairs, drying her eyes with a piece of rag. But it was difficult. She couldn't stop crying, and she didn't want her father to see her tears.

"Please don't forsake me, my love!" Mikael shouted down the stairs.

But she didn't turn back to face him. She walked

away, a sorrowful figure in the near darkness.

Mikael's voice echoed around the wooden beams and low ceiling. He slammed his fist into the wall, punching a hole right through the weak mortar. He ran back into the bedroom, shut the door behind him then collapsed to the floor, crying. Would he really never see his dear, sweet Maria again? He gripped onto the ruffles of his white shirt. His heart was hurting. He felt inconsolable, feeling the agony rip through his heart.

"My Maria!" He suddenly perked up, having an idea. He tore the locket from around his neck and threw it onto the bed. He rushed over to the writing bureau in the corner of the room. He grabbed a quill and dipped it into a glass bottle of black ink. Ruffling through the drawer of the bureau, he found a piece of paper and scribbled a note upon it:

My darling Maria,

I have enclosed my golden locket within this paper, the golden royal locket from my father that means everything to me. I am giving it to you. That is how much I wish to express my love for you. If you ever change your mind and wish to visit me my home country of Sweden, then please sell this locket and use it as financial means to travel there. If you decide otherwise, then please use it to fund your life here. If I can't have you in this life then we will be reunited in the next. I know this for a fact.

Soulmates are meant to be together.

Love always, Mikael.

Mikael waited for the ink to dry and placed the locket in the middle. He folded the edges of the paper over it, making it into a small parcel before tying a thread of cotton around it. He looked across the room, at the loose floorboard they used as a means for leaving notes and gifts to each other during their ongoing secret relationship. He placed it inside and replaced the floorboard, pulling the rug back over it.

Min Maria...

Even though she hadn't physically left, Lizzie felt her own sense of self returning, back to the present day, to the present moment, to the more modern room before her.

"My Maria," she sobbed, emotions of heartbreak still overwhelming her. She felt such anguish at having to relive her most heartbreaking memory of losing the love of her life in such vivid detail. She groped around her neck for the locket that was no longer there.

Heading to the hiding spot, she was disappointed to find it covered with carpets and furniture. She winced at the noise of the chest of drawers as she pulled it away from the wall. She still wasn't in her right mind after her strange experience, so she pulled the carpet up, straining to prise it up with her fingernails. She yanked up the underlay and pulled it over to one side to reveal the floorboards. The floorboard still wasn't fixed down properly. She smiled as she pulled it up, peering down into the dark crevice. She almost didn't see it at first until she used the light from her mobile phone to illuminate the dark space.

"I don't believe it!" she gasped. Seeing the small parcel was unbelievable, solid proof that her past life experience had been real. She reached inside and took hold of it, jittering as a large, scared spider ran over her hand.

She blew the many layers of thick dust off the parcel and peered at it anxiously, excitedly, opening it out, reading the handwriting word for word.

Love always, Mikael.

She clasped the locket tightly in her hand before placing it around her neck. Feeling amazed, she folded the paper up and put it into her handbag. She replaced the carpet and chest of drawers, hoping nobody would notice. She sat down with a thump on the bed and tried to fathom the surreal night, how she had somehow relived a scene from her past life, an echo of time contained within the walls of the building. But she knew it was more than that. It wasn't just a time slip. She had managed to relieve the memories of her past life as a Swedish prince in the late 1800s.

But why now? Was this a crucial point in her life journey in which she needed to learn a life lesson? Deep down, she knew it was. She knew exactly why. Her relationship with Paul was on the rocks. Her wish to move to Sweden had pushed him over the edge, perhaps awakened distant feelings within him, distant memories. It was history repeating itself. She couldn't allow them to break up. Not again. Her eyelids began to close. Feeling exhausted, she lay down, still clutching the love note in her hand. She felt herself falling sleep.

* * *

"Did you sleep well?" Mike asked as Lizzie checked out early. She smiled as she handed him the key.

"I slept wonderfully, thank you, Mike."

"You didn't hear any ghostly voices then?"

"Not a thing," she fibbed. "Tell me, though, the prince from the tavern sign, he was the prince the place was named after?"

"Aye, Prince Mikael Havstam, the youngest of the young Swedish princes in the late 1800s. He used to stay here as a rest point before going on to the royal palaces. He was a very kind man, very popular with locals as he never flaunted his wealth and had a great sense of humour. He always dressed down and gave money to the poor. The locals would do anything to defend him, protecting him from the vagabonds that often tried to mug him. I'm not sure why he stayed here in particular, though. Bit of a lowly place for a royal, isn't it?"

"Perhaps he had a lover here."

"There's nothing about that in the local history

records." Mike stroked his beard contemplatively.

"It's just an idea," she grinned. "Do you know what happened to him?"

"I read that he moved back to Sweden permanently. For some reason he never returned back here. In 1879 the pub was renamed from The Bard's Inn in to The Prince's Tavern in his honour."

"Did he ever marry?"

"Yeah, he had three or four wives from what I know. Had seven children. Only had one daughter, though. A girl."

"Named Maria?"

"Yeah, you are a local history buff, aren't you?"

Lizzie smirked. "And what about the maids here? I heard that there was also a maid called Maria here at about the same time the prince used to stay. She was the owner's daughter. Do you think they could be connected?"

"Ah, I have no idea. It's a long shot, but it's a possibility," he mused, rubbing his beard, obviously enjoying the banter. "I don't really know. I'd have to trawl the archives. There wasn't much about a maid in the local history books. I guess the maids weren't of much importance to the local historians. "

Lizzie looked at him sharply. "Maybe not to some historians, but to history itself, I think maids are most definitely important." She smiled awkwardly, not wanting to get too animated about it.

"I suppose," Mike shrugged.

"Anyway, I must shoot. Thank you."

"You're welcome. Thank you for your custom. I hope you will stay here again sometime."

"I will. I'll bring my boyfriend next time." She shook his hand and said her goodbyes.

She felt a huge relief as she walked away from the tavern, feeling the heavy shroud of history lift from her. She felt certain that the voices would no longer plague the building and its guests now that they had been required by their rightful owner. She wondered what other histories loomed in the aether of the walls, what memories from the deep recesses of time had been impressed upon them, what stories and long-lost lives were encoded onto the present day, just out of reach of our mortal perception.

She rang in sick at work and headed straight home to see Paul. She knocked on the door instead of using her key. As soon as he opened the front door, she threw herself into his arms.

"Woah, hello!" he said, still looking a bit grumpy, but smiling from her exuberant greeting.

"I've missed you!" She kissed him. Even though she'd tried to quickly dry her work suit with a hair dryer that morning, it was still a little damp, and she was still tired, but she was energised with excitement and affection.

"I thought you would've been pleased to get away from me," he scowled at first, but then warmed to her jovial mood.

"That's not true."

"Why aren't you at work?" he asked, making a

cup of tea at the kitchen counter.

"Rang in sick. I wanted to spend the day with you instead," she smiled as she placed her arms around his waist and hugged him from behind.

"You? Mrs. Workaholic pulled a sickie? Well, I am proud."

Lizzie let go of him and took her heels off, slumping down on the living room sofa. "When I was gone it made me realise just how much you mean to me. I'm sorry that I just assumed that you would just up-sticks and move your whole life just for me. It was unfair and I apologise."

Paul sulked for a moment but then sighed. "I'm sorry I overreacted. I don't want you to miss a fantastic opportunity. For some reason, I just had this deep, horrible feeling that it would be the end of us, and I couldn't bear it," he said, putting down the mugs onto the side table. He then took her in his arms and kissed her head.

"This time it won't be the end of us. We'll discuss it." She gripped his hand tightly. It was then that she saw the deep ridge on his temple. It hadn't come to mind last night in the heat of the moment.

"This time?"

"How did you get that scar again?"

Paul rubbed his head. "I don't know, I think I was just born like it," he shrugged. He offered her one of the mugs of steaming hot tea, which she gratefully accepted, taking a huge mouthful.

"Did you know that people are often born with

birthmarks that resemble injuries from a past life?"

"Can't say I did."

She chuckled at his puzzled expression, staring into his eyes. The same hazel eyes as Maria's stared back. She knew they were lovers in a past life, reunited in this life to sort out their differences. Mikael had been right that they would have another chance to be together. She always knew they were soulmates.

"Huh?" Paul wrinkled his nose, smiling at her eccentricity.

"Well, when we met I felt an instant connection, like we'd already known each other forever."

"Me too. Maybe we were lovers in a past life."

She smiled, enclosing one hand around the locket she was wearing.

"Where did you get that necklace from? Have I seen it before? It looks familiar," he asked, sipping at his hot tea.

Lizzie grinned at him and shoved her hand into her handbag, taking out the love note from Mikael.

"I've got a story to tell you, my love."

GYPERIA 2138

I couldn't wait to get back home so I could relax. I'd had a long day at the factory. My body was aching all over from working so hard, not to mention the cold I'd had all week. I was so exhausted I could barely propel my body down the road. My comfortable bed awaited me, with a steaming hot cup of tea and a few biscuits.

"Ten minutes and you'll be home, Anabelle," I said out loud. "Just ten minutes," I told my weary legs. I couldn't wait to take my uncomfortable work clothes off and change into my comfortable pyjamas. I threw my long, blonde ponytail over my shoulder and hoisted my backpack more securely onto my shoulder.

I sniffled, wiping my runny nose with a tissue, and started to think about my boring life. "Ugh, Malverton," I huffed, stuffing the tissue into my pocket. I was so sick of Malverton. Every single day I walked this boring route to and from work. Nothing interesting ever happened in my hometown of Malverton. It was pleasant in a safe, boring way, although its atmosphere was as dull as the grey clouds that rolled overhead.

I walked on the pavement around a roundabout. There wasn't much traffic about. The area was shrouded with a wall of tall conifer trees, obscuring the small winding path which I was about to take. I always cut through the park which led to the main town.

As I walked down the road from the first exit of the roundabout, the roofs of two buildings emerged from behind the tall trees. I realised that those buildings weren't there before. How could they be? That's where the park was situated.

I stared at them in awe as I walked closer. A strange feeling made the pit of my stomach ache. I felt queasy. How could I have never seen these magnificent buildings before? There was no way I could have blindly walked past the loud noises and sights of a construction site every day. I know my attention was usually lost in my imagination, but that seemed unfeasible. There was simply no way that these buildings could have popped up overnight.

After about a minute, I had walked down the winding path that cut between the trees and emerged onto what looked like a car park of a large, strange-looking shopping centre, except there were no cars parked on it.

I stopped in dismay, feeling a hot prickly panic stab at my senses. Where had the park gone? There was never a shopping centre here before.

Instead of the children's play area, wooden tables and then stretches of grass and trees, there was now a sort of retail park. The buildings looked very unfamiliar, a bizarre mixture of old-fashioned and futuristic-looking buildings. A couple of buildings at the far end looked vaguely familiar, but they had been derelict Victorian estates on the other side of the park. They had now been renovated in a futuristic manner.

"There's just no way…" I stopped and stared. I had walked through the park just this morning. None of this was here then.

One of the buildings was covered in reflective glass panels and the other was colourful with a large billboard advertising a product I'd never heard of before. They both sported colourful neon signage in cursive handwriting that showed they were retail outlets of some sort.

"What the hell?" I gaped up at the looming structures. I continued to walk towards them, walking faster now in an effort to reach them and satisfy my curiosity.

Something wasn't right. Something in the air just didn't feel right. Everything looked brighter than usual. I realised it was because everything was so clean. The reflection of the glass panels of the buildings glinted in the air, reflecting light over the car park. The floor was paved with strange tiles that felt rubbery underfoot.

There were people walking around on their daily business. They looked perfectly comfortable with their surroundings. It was just me freaking out.

"What the hell is going on?" I said to myself. My curiosity and shock were the only things stopping a panic attack from setting in.

There was a large tunnel made from an opaque

Perspex material. With the weak sunlight reflecting off it, it was tinted slightly bluish white. This open tunnel appeared to lead into the entrance of the shopping centre.

"Excuse me," I said to the nearest person walking by, a man who looked to be in late thirties. He was wearing a black suit and hat, and carrying a briefcase. Although he was wearing formal attire, his shirt and tie were loose, so he looked more casual.

"What?" he answered abruptly. He seemed shocked that I had stopped him, as if it was terribly rude to do so. His accent sounded foreign, kind of Russian.

"I just wondered where this retail park has come from. I've never seen it before. Has it only recently been built?" I know it sounded ridiculous, as if such a huge construction could have been erected in such a short space of time, but I was at a loss for an explanation.

The man sighed loudly. "I guess you're not from around here. This retail park has been here for decades." He went to walk away and continue across the car park.

"What? Here in Malverton?" I stopped him again, desperate for answers.

He stopped dead in his tracks. "Malverton…" He stared into the distance as if trying to recall a fact. One side of his mouth curled into a wry smile.

"Yes, Malverton."

"Haven't heard it called that in years. The area

did used to be called Malverton, but that was about eighty years ago at least, way before I was even born. Why are you calling the district by its old town's name?"

My eyes went wide. "Because this *is* Malverton. So where am I now? If this is not Malverton, then where the hell am I?" I became rather agitated.

The smile dropped from his face. "You youngsters. Stop fooling around. I have to get to work," he grunted, trying to push past me.

"Look, I'm sorry to stop you, but please, just tell me. I don't know what's happening here. What do you mean, *district*?" I pleaded for answers.

The man saw my distress and sighed. "You are in Gyperia. Malverton and its neighbouring towns all became Gyperia around 75 years ago when England combined with Russia to become one nation. You know, after the end of the third world war with Colonia, which used to be known as America," he explained in a pedantic manner, as if humouring my lack of knowledge of world events.

"War?" I felt a hot panic flush through me.

"Yes. The terrible nuclear war of 2053. It reduced the world's population by almost a third. When it became common knowledge that America's president, David Monagan, was exploiting the carnage in the Middle East to gain power over Europe and the rest of the world, England and Russia teamed up and became the forerunners in the fight to beat him and the oppressive one world government he had intended to implement onto us. That's when America nuked Russia. Russia fired back. In retaliation, the world was devastated by nuclear war. That damn President Monagan. He was such a cold bastard. With Asia's backing, we nuked America back, sending their nation back to the dark ages. That's why it's now known as Colonia, because they have only just begun to rebuild their nation from its ashes. It took decades to recover our separate nations and the environment, but we managed to rebuild our world again, and our health, although we're still feeling the harsh effects of the nuclear fallout today. It's common knowledge. It's history. I don't understand how you don't know all this."

I stared at him like he was the mad man spouting crazy tales. I swallowed hard as the reality of the situation dawned on me with full force. He was telling the truth. No wonder he had a Russian accent.

"What year is it?" I needed confirmation of the obvious.

"2138," he stated casually.

Hot prickles of fear ran through my body. My head began to spin. I felt dizzy. I had somehow travelled 120 years into the future, into a post-nuclear, post-world-war-three world.

"What year did you think it was?" He raised his eyebrows.

"2018," I managed to mouth, staring at the floor, feeling numb with shock.

Understandably, he looked at me like I was crazy.

He snorted in amusement, or perhaps in pity.

"Going way back there, kiddo. Back to the dark old days when everyone lived in ignorance and oppression. Thankfully, times have changed. Anyway, I'd better be off." He began to walk away again, towards an underground entrance on the far-right side of the car park. Perhaps it led to a transport system, like a railway or tube service.

I stood there in silence, trying to digest all of the information he had just given me. It sounded like a ridiculous conspiracy theory from a science fiction plot or an internet forum, and although it seemed fairly plausible, I didn't want to accept that I had travelled forwards in time, into the middle of the next century. Had I been blessed or cursed to see the future?

The man kept looking back at me as he walked away. He walked up to a man ominously traversing the car park. The man looked like a security guard, wearing a uniform and holding a walkie-talkie-like device. I saw the suited man talk to the guard in hurried whispers then peer over in my direction.

The guard spoke for a few moments into his walkie-talkie and then began to stride towards me.

"You okay there, ma'am?" he asked. His accent also had a Russian lilt to it.

"I, er…" I felt flustered, panicked, but I didn't want to show it. I glared at the suited man for betraying me and then peered up at the concerned guard.

"What's your name, ma'am?"

"Anabelle," I replied. My voice was shaky.

"Can you tell me what's wrong, Anabelle?"

I didn't want to sound crazy, so I decided to go with a safer story than time travel. "I think I have amnesia," I said quietly to him. It was the first idea that came to mind.

He placed an arm around me, ushering me towards the large opaque tunnel. "But the man over there said you thought Gyperia was still called Malverton and that the year was 2018."

"I'm obviously mistaken." I looked back to see the suited man scurrying down the entrance to the transport system, back on schedule of his daily business of 2138. I must have been a crazy inconvenience to him. Just some nutter.

"Well, don't worry, ma'am. There's a medical facility here that can help you. It has specialised doctors that know how to treat amnesia and all sorts of stuff. They'll help you," he said with genuine concern in his voice.

I didn't know what to say. I just wanted to get back home, back to my time, but I knew that if I flipped out and acted crazy then the outcome wouldn't fare well for me. I'd be contained and locked up here or worse, trapped in a future I wasn't meant to know about. I wondered what mystical or scientific process had caused this event, this time slip. Just fifteen minutes ago I was having a mundane day in 2018. Then somehow, I'd just walked down the road straight into another century. The numbness of my shock helped in maintaining a false sense of calm.

"This way, ma'am," the guard steered me through the tunnel. The inside of the shopping centre was very clean, very futuristic-looking. There were rows of entrances on each side that led into the shops that lined the outside. The signage above them was identical to the neon signage on the building exteriors. It was an attractive retail and business centre, with all of the cleanliness, visions of hospitality and mod-cons you'd expect from a future time. Holographic signs displayed current news and adverts promoting objects for sale. There were lots of people walking around, chatting and shopping.

I wanted to stop and stare and try to take in all of the details of future products and events, and people that weren't even born yet, but the guard was ushering me down a clinical-looking corridor towards a stainless steel door.

"Here we are." The guard had his arm around my shoulders as he knocked on the door of the medical facility.

"Enter," a voice came from the inside of the room.

The heavily insulated door clicked to unlock. The guard pushed the door open and let me walk through first. I jumped out of my skin as a sudden noise of pressurised air escaped and a stream of cool, tingly air shot down at us.

I gasped, shrieking, throwing myself against the

172

guard in alarm. "What was that?" I asked in dismay, staring up at the ceiling. There was a row of metal studs imbedded into the top of the doorframe. The pressurised air must have come from them.

"Don't worry, it's just an antibacterial air refresher. It detects and neutralises any dangerous germs. It's just normal protocol for a medical centre. You're acting like you've never been in one before," the guard quizzed me, eyebrows raised. I noticed the door had closed behind us.

I turned to see three male doctors staring quizzically at me. They were all wearing protective gloves and had face masks strapped under their chins. I felt queasy again. My hands had started to tremble.

"Doctor Fisher, Anabelle here has been having some problems with her memory and some confusion about what year it is," the guard offered.

"Hmm. Please sit here," Fisher replied, motioning towards a padded light blue chair. Fisher looked to be in his early fifties; a small, bearded and moustached man with a no-nonsense expression etched onto his face.

I cautiously headed towards the chair, regarding the futuristic medical equipment around the room. "Will you wait outside for me? Please," I pleaded with the guard as I gingerly sat down on the comfortable chair that did nothing to comfort me. I sat rigidly. My whole body was tense with anxiety. I nervously gripped onto my bag with both arms.

He saw my distress and nodded. "I'll just be

outside," he assured me, then left the facility. He opened the door then promptly closed it behind him. Was he placating me, the crazy woman, or was he being genuine?

"Please relax," Fisher said as he pulled a large transparent dome over my head. It looked like one of those hair drying domes you get in hair salons, except I could see through it. I jumped as he attached a strange clamp to my index finger. It connected to a wire which connected to a computer.

"What is this machine?" I frowned, peering up at the dome.

"This contraption will read your neural activity so we can determine what the problem is." He spoke to me like I was a child, or as if I was dumb. I guess I had just 'lost my memory'.

"So it's kinda like an fMRI machine? It's very small for one of those," I replied, puffing my cheeks out.

"Yes. A functional magnetic resonance imaging machine..." He looked so surprised that his moustache twitched. I felt incredibly tense and uneasy. I wanted to hurry up and get out of here somehow. I wanted to return to 2018.

"Neural activity is the electrical signals passed through synapses in your brain. Thoughts, in other words," he stated, tapping some things into the computer to get it fired up to record my brainwaves.

"I know what neural activity is. Just because I work in a factory doesn't mean I'm stupid!" I snapped at him, sick of him patronising my intelligence, realising I was overreacting due to my own complexes and not feeling great from my cold, not to mention this weird situation.

He seemed surprised, coughing loudly at my rebuttal.

I peered around the room, at the other doctors watching. One chuckled, as if he was amused by my response.

"A factory? How absurd! Young women no longer work in factories." Fisher raised his eyebrows.

Crap. I didn't know what future young people did.

"So, Anabelle, what year do you think it is?"

"I don't *think* it's any year. I *know* that the year is 2138," I replied.

"But only ten minutes ago it was reported that you thought the year was 2018," he raised his eyebrows, surveying my response.

I watched the 3D model of my brain in live time on the computer screen. It was a really fancy, advanced fMRI scan. I wondered how the machine was relatively silent compared to the usual whirring and humming they produced. I was amazed how it had scanned my brain so quickly, but then I remembered that this was futuristic technology. There were levels at the side monitoring other neurological and chemical functions and I guessed the clamp on my finger was measuring my physiological responses. It was fascinating. I'd always wanted to see what my brain looked like, to see how it worked. Even though I worked in a factory, I was really into science. I didn't want to work there forever. It was just to tide me over until something better came along. Well, that's what I kept telling myself. I was only twenty-seven. I still had time to forge out a new career path.

"Write all this down, Petrov," Fisher said to another doctor stood next to the monitor. Petrov was thin, tall and very pale. He looked a lot younger than Fisher and the other doctor, probably late teens or early twenties. He nodded, writing things down onto a notepad in regard to these levels.

"I, er... was confused." I knew it was a rubbish answer and I knew they were already deeply suspicious of me. The icy tone in the room and the suspicious glares proved that.

"Retrograde amnesia is a possibility, but you still wouldn't have any memories of this area from over a hundred years ago because you weren't alive then," Fisher sighed, sounding puzzled.

"Brain scan shows no damaged neural pathways. There is no evidence of amnesia, lesions or trauma found," Petrov certified. He sounded Russian. "Apart from high levels of anxiety and adrenaline, the brain is in healthy, full working order."

"What's your full name?" Fisher asked.

"Anabelle Davis," I replied.

"And your age?"

"27."

"Your birthdate?"

Shit. I couldn't say I was born in 1991. That would make me 147 years old. I quickly tried to subtract 27 from 2138, but my brain too was inflamed by panic and confusion to do basic sums. Red spikes appeared on the monitor and red blips pulsated along the blue 3D neural pathways.

"I thought this was a brain scan, not a lie detector," I frowned, feeling worry prickle at me.

"Please just answer the question."

"The twelfth of June, 2111?" I answered uncertainly.

"The last response indicates she's lying. Massive spike in anxiety and a change in chemical levels. The entrance scanner also detected unknown pathogens on her being. It ran them through the genetic archive..." Petrov coughed, looking furtive, then fell silent.

"And?" Fisher pressed him.

"The pathogen is from a strain of the common cold that was virulent throughout the 20th and 21st centuries. Fortunately, it was obliterated during the nuclear war. Of course, viral pathogens have evolved since then. But this specific strain is archaic. It simply cannot exist today..." he trailed off.

I peered sheepishly around the room. The doctors gawked at me like I was a fetid creature from the swamp. They exchanged furtive glances. The elephant in the room was trumpeting the obvious: that I was not from this time.

They all quickly pulled their masks onto their faces. "Perhaps someone has somehow found a sample of the strain of the archaic common cold and has somehow reintroduced it. This could be a case of bio-warfare. This could cause chaos. We'll have to keep this woman on lockdown," Fisher whispered the last sentence to his colleagues, but I heard every word.

"Lockdown? What? Bio-warfare? No! It's just a cold!" I protested, my head swimming with anxiety. My brain scan was doing all sorts of weird visuals.

"Give me your bag," Fisher demanded, holding his gloved hand out.

"No." I clutched onto it tightly, knowing that I had ID in my purse and other things that would expose me as being an unintended time traveller. I shook my head.

He reached out and tried to grab the bag from me. I resisted, but he managed to wrestle it from my grip. He opened the zip with gloved hands and emptied the contents onto a clean white surface. The doctors all clamoured around to view its contents.

Any moment now, they would find definite proof that I was from 2018. I had visions of being detained and experimented on. I felt another hot wave of anxiety flush through me. I was becoming light-headed. As I became panicked, the blue brain model was rapidly turning red and the monitor levels were going crazy.

"I could have a weapon in there," I retorted, trying to sound threatening, although my voice was trembling with fear.

"Apart from the cold, the entrance scanner

detected no weapons or any possible chemical bombs," Petrov stated. He tried to maintain a detached, professional tone, but his voice was quivering with excitement.

There was a moment of silence as the doctors picked through my belongings like medical magpies, attempting to find the golden nuggets of evidence to take back to the nest of their bosses — priceless treasures to show what good pets they were to their owners.

Fisher picked up a newly opened packet of Polo mints. He turned the spherical tube with his fingers to examine it. "Paper and foil packaging. What an odd combination." He sniffed the packet. "Smells like peppermint. Polo. Anyone ever heard of it?"

Petrov and the other doctor grumbled, shaking their heads.

"There might be something in the archive about it. But if it's a pre-war brand then who knows. Maybe she is from 2018..." Petrov glared at me suspiciously, with complete fascination.

I swallowed hard.

"We could just ask her," the doctor who had remained silent up until this point spoke up. This was all so bizarre, seeing something as popular and common as a packet of Polos treated with such fascination, like it was an alien object from outer space.

Fisher then found my purse. He took out my money and debit cards. Excited chatter filled the room as they examined the notes, holding them up to the light to see the illuminated image of Queen Elizabeth. They scrutinised the coins like they were ancient, like the excitement an archaeologist gets from unearthing long-lost treasures.

"This is crazy." Fisher pressed a button and spoke into an intercom on the wall. "Code U! Get Stanley in here *now*!" His voice was trembling with excitement. He then traipsed back over to the computer desk, pressed a button on it, and the door popped open.

The guard walked in.

"Get Stanley!" Fisher roared at the guard. "We have a Code U here — an *unidentifiable*."

The guard's eyes went wide. He was staring in bemusement at the items from my bag.

The doctors were so bemused with my belongings that they weren't aware the guard had carelessly left the door open. They weren't even looking at me, too occupied by my anachronistic belongings.

I took my chance.

I pushed the dome up, ripped the clamp off my finger then got up and ran straight for the door. With all my might, I butted my shoulder into the guard and he went flying to the ground.

Alarms started ringing overhead and the doctors were shouting angrily. All I could concentrate on was escaping. I turned back after I'd cleared the corridor. The doctors and guard were chasing after me. I hurtled through the brightly lit shopping centre, heading back the way I had come in.

"GET HER! Get my unidentifiable back! You are so fired for this. You will never work in Gyperia again!" I heard Fisher yelling at the guard. Heavy footsteps thudded behind me.

I was met with the full force of two shoppers. We rolled around the floor, entwined in a mass of shopping bags and limbs. I pushed myself up, not caring for them.

I could see the bright light of the exit in the distance. My legs were aching, my body was covered in sweat, and I barely had any energy, but I ran like I had never ran before, straight towards the bright light. I emerged outside, back onto the rubbery tiles. A few people on their daily business were alerted to the commotion. The cool air made me sneeze. I slowed momentarily, feeling faint. I sneezed again, wiping my nose on my sleeve.

"Don't let her spread the common cold! It's been eradicated. This is a nightmare! Capture her!" Fisher yelled. They were close behind me now. He slowed, pulling his mask tighter to his face, as if he was scared to get near me.

I took off again, running towards the large conifer trees. It seemed a long shot, but perhaps if I went back the way I had emerged then I might be able to go back to 2018.

Or I might be stuck here forever.

There was only one way to find out.

I ran and I ran, through the trees, out onto a

pavement. I could see a roundabout!

The air suddenly changed, felt different.

The shouting and footsteps had vanished.

I was back in Malverton.

Good old, boring Malverton.

I stopped and turned towards the conifer trees. I could no longer see the protruding roofs of the strange futuristic buildings, just a cloudy grey sky. A usual dull day in Malverton.

How wonderful!

My chest was heaving, my heart was thudding, and my body was drenched with sweat. I could barely regain my breath as I stared, waiting for the doctors and guard to come running through.

I waited a few minutes.

But nobody came.

I imagined them running down the path to find I had disappeared. I imagined them cursing, mortified they had lost their *unidentifiable*. I imagined the guard getting berated and fired. I envisioned them putting the retail park on lockdown to contain the germs of the archaic common cold. I imagined them keeping my cheap personal items; my Polos, money and phone as priceless pre-war artefacts.

I imagined a lot of things. I knew what the future held. My mind boggled. The prospect of a future nuclear war absolutely terrified me, but I was too exhausted to think about it at that moment.

After a few minutes, I finally got my breath back. The sweat had dried on my clammy skin. The familiarity of the dull weather and the smell of exhaust emissions comforted me.

I was back in Malverton, 2018. And that's where I wanted to stay.

THE CONDUIT

The alien craft was a wondrous sight to behold. The seamless metal it was crafted from appeared luminous from the many flashing white lights reflecting from its base.

Cate typed out the scene she was imagining. Her mind always raced faster than her fingers, but they desperately tried to keep up, clacking across the keyboard as she typed out the ideas that were pouring into her mind.

Getting a burst of inspiration felt enormously fulfilling. Sometimes the slump of 'writer's block' would last for days, for weeks, for months, when she just didn't want to write anything at all. And then there were other times when she felt fired up, positively brimming with enthusiasm and excitement, using every precious second to zone out and pen a story.

This was one of those times.

She sat at the kitchen table, hands racing across her laptop keyboard. She'd zoned out, staring at the screen, at the words forming alongside the visions in her head. Her tongue perched against the roof of her dry mouth. She was too engrossed in her work to reach out to the full glass of water sitting next to her laptop. If she reached out to have a swig, she would most likely lose her flow, and she couldn't have that.

"Do you want a cup of tea?" her mother, Gwen, asked her. Cate hadn't even noticed her enter the kitchen.

"No thanks," Cate mumbled automatically, lifting her head slightly, but keeping her eyes and mind directly attached to her work.

"Coffee?"

"Nah."

"Okay, well I'll put the kettle on anyway." Gwen proceeded to fill the kettle with water.

Not that Cate had noticed. She had zoned out all external stimuli. She typed even faster. As she neared the end of the passage, she added a few extra thoughts and lines into some paragraphs. Finally, she sat back and smiled.

It was complete.

Cate realised that she did in fact want a cup of tea. She quickly grabbed the glass of water and took a few mouthfuls to lubricate her dry mouth. She got up from the wooden table chair and stretched out her limbs.

"Ow." She gripped her back. Being completely absorbed in her writing, she hadn't noticed the uncomfortable position she'd been sitting in for the last couple of hours. She traipsed over to her mum who was filling up the teapot with boiling hot water.

"Sorry, mum. I will have a cuppa actually." She

put an arm around her and kissed her on the cheek.

"Thought you would want one," Gwen smiled, stirring the pot before placing the tea cosy atop it.

"I don't mean to ignore you when I'm writing, but if I don't hang on to the moments where I can fully concentrate and I'm not distracted by anything, then I'd never get any work done."

"I understand, love. You need to get your second book done after all."

"I know," Cate grinned. She pushed her fingers through her voluminous mane of hair and pulled it up into a ponytail. Sometimes it was a pain to groom but she felt it was one of her best features. She felt fortunate to have inherited her tiny mother's English Rose features and proud of her hair and eyes from her African father. She was tall and slim like her father, and chatty and wild like her mother. She'd inherited stubbornness and feistiness from both parents, however.

"I can't believe how my debut novel took off. It ranked number seventeen in the science fiction charts on Amazon last week," Cate beamed, messing with her nose ring, a small metallic hoop decorating her right nostril.

"I dunno where you get the ideas from, all of those aliens and technological things. I don't have a clue about all that stuff. Some of the words you use… it's way over my head," Gwen said as she impatiently stirred the teapot again to strengthen the brewing tea inside.

"The ideas just pop into my mind. They're so intense and vivid. I feel like I'm actually there, like I'm experiencing it myself. Sometimes I wonder if it is actually just my imagination or if I'm channelling an external knowledge or something. I'm not sure which would be weirder, that my brain is structured in such a way to create these fantastical and deranged ideas or if my brain is some sort of conduit to divine information from elsewhere."

"I don't know about that. You're a smart girl. I'm proud of you."

"Thanks, Mum," Cate smiled. "It sure beats getting a proper job."

Gwen laughed. "Well, you did try, but this is better. Your father worked in a factory for thirty years. I was a cleaner for twenty-five years. Thankless jobs. We're glad that you don't have to do that. It's a hard life. Stick with your writing. You can do what you want, when you want, and be your own boss."

"Which suits me just fine. At least I get to work from home." She peered down at her clothes. She was slumming it in a loose-fitting, short-sleeved top, pyjama trousers and fluffy slippers. They were comfy as hell. This was her writer's uniform. Most of her friends had their own families, great jobs and owned their own houses. Cate had never dated anyone worth moving in with and hadn't had much luck financially until her recent bestseller. She was nearly thirty, still living at home with her retired parents. But she was fine with it. She loved spending time with them. The majority of her days were spent in her pyjamas, drinking her bodyweight in tea, and writing like her life depended on it.

What a life. I'm such a professional, she thought, trying not to laugh.

"Looks like a nice spring evening," Gwen remarked.

Cate peered out of the kitchen window. It was still light out. "It does. I'm gonna go sit outside in the garden and get some fresh air for a while. Wanna sit with me?"

"Sure. I'll bring the tea outside."

"Lovely," Cate smiled. She strolled out into the garden. The evening air offered a refreshing breeze. It felt wonderful to relax after intense writing periods. Being absorbed in imaginary worlds and scenes often left her feeling exhausted and disconnected from reality. She hoped the fresh wind would wake her up from her writer's reverie. She often loved to sit in the garden in the evenings. She wondered what beautiful combination of colours the atmosphere would paint tonight. She loved watching the wavelengths of light change the colours of the sky as the night progressed, from light blue to dusky orange, to dusky blue and then to black, before staring wistfully up at the stars for hours.

She noticed her ginger cat, Tomkins, padding over to her.

"Come here, furry butt." She wiggled her fingers near the ground to beckon him over.

Tomkins trotted over and then suddenly stopped in his tracks, staring around in a startled manner.

"I said come here." She went to grab him, but he arched his back and hissed at her. He then darted off like his life depended on it, jumping over the fence and disappearing.

"Hmm, that's not like him." She felt insulted at the attitude of her usually lovable pet.

Cate stood in the garden waiting for her mum to come out. An eerie sense of paranoia suddenly prickled at her senses. She felt uncomfortable, like someone or something was watching her. Not even the warm evening air felt pleasant enough to relax her. Something odd and out of place in the sky caught her attention, something moving at the edge of the clouds.

She stared up to see something moving in a fashion that seemed unnatural.

A UFO? Am I finally seeing a real god damn UFO? she thought to herself.

Her suspicions were confirmed when a massive alien spaceship suddenly blinked into view, appearing within the clear area of the sky. It was as if it had materialised from nowhere, like it had been cloaked, hiding out in plain sight. It set her nerves on end to think she had been staring at something invisible, with the prickly sense of awareness that something was amiss, a sixth sense of perception, but her eyes had been deceiving her otherwise.

She felt numb with a mixture of sheer fear, wonder, curiosity and amazement. She stood rooted to the spot, staring intently at the spaceship. It was probably the most beautiful thing she had ever seen, made even more magnificent and terrifying because it was something so advanced and alien. She couldn't comprehend its size. It was so vast, but it moved with such grace, agility and silence that it glided through the clouds without interrupting anything in its path. The world below seemed unaware of its presence, save for a few birds chirruping fervently at the disturbance.

She stared up at its base. The seamless metal it was crafted from appeared luminous from the many flashing white lights reflecting from its base. She wondered why it needed that many lights. They were irregular and were in no sort of order that made any sense to her.

Wait, I remember typing that...

The thought suddenly dawned on her, why this craft looked so familiar. It was familiar. She had written about this exact spaceship in her stories many times, when the ideas had just come to her, during the times it felt like her brain had been channelling a divine inspiration.

This thing from my stories is real? How am I connected to it? Am I really a conduit of information?

As she struggled to process the situation in her mind, the lights began to move away from the ship and the metal panels rotated in on themselves, round and inwards, whirring and whizzing with metallic clangs. The noise grated on her, causing her to realise the fear that had been overwhelmed by her sheer curiosity. And when she saw the huge spherical panel in the base's centre begin to glow a radiating red hue, she froze in terror.

Somehow, base instinct took over and she managed to shock herself out of her reverie. She dashed towards the house like her life depended on it.

Gwen had just taken a step outside.

"Quick, get back into the house!" Cate yelled urgently to her, gasping because she was out of breath.

"Why? What's wrong?" Gwen asked, worried.

"The aliens have come to take me again," she cried, straining her neck upwards to the sky. A vague feeling came to her senses, how the aliens had taken her many times before, but it felt like trying to bring forth a distant memory or a dream she couldn't recollect.

"What?" Gwen blinked in dismay.

The spherical panel had turned from a glowing red to a hot white and was beginning to stream down an energy beam right at Cate. She felt her body being transported before the beam had even directly touched her. A strong wind whipped around the garden, causing a few plant pots to fall over and smash, and a flurry of foliage to twist in the gust. She gripped onto the side of their stone bench in an attempt to stay grounded, but her feet were being lifted up from the ground. Her stomach lurched upwards, like that was being pulled up first, through her body, like her whole cells were being lifted in a slightly disarranged order, which was an incredibly uncomfortable sensation.

"Oh, my god," Gwen mouthed as she saw her daughter levitating in the air. She stood speechless, mouth agape as she finally saw the spaceship. Cate managed to thrust herself forwards, falling out of the energy beam, and lurching to the ground.

"Quick, in the house!" Cate shouted, shoving her mum forwards. Gwen dropped the tray of tea and biscuits on the floor. They ran inside, but she knew resistance was futile. She knew she was kidding herself thinking she'd be safe inside. The aliens possessed technology that could remain undisturbed and undetected as it navigated through mere brick and mortar, through physical matter like it was air or water. She knew that. She knew things about them from her stories. She felt deeply disturbed beyond rational thought.

How can the horrible things I imagined actually be true?

With bated breath, she waited a few seconds for the inevitable. There was a bright flash of white light and she felt the sensation of movement through the air, of a cellular transportation rather than a whole bodily one.

Where am I?

She must have blacked out because she didn't remember flying up through the air. Her consciousness had felt very heavy during the transit. She now had a major headache and she felt displaced and sore all over.

Cate stared around. She was in a room full of other people. People that must have been abducted and physically manifested inside of the ship. They were all sitting in a group on the floor. They all looked terrified, hugging each other and crying. Her mother was there, too, sitting amongst them.

"Mum!" Cate winced, rubbing her sore head.

Gwen looked distraught. "Wh-what's going on?" she stammered.

"I'm not sure." Cate was suddenly distracted by the room. It appeared to be a sort of engine room. Why would the spaceship need an engine room when it didn't run in the conventional sense? The ship didn't run on conventional energy. That would be ludicrous.

This isn't right.

Cate then saw the aliens that were standing around the abductees. They were grey aliens, the type that have adorned science fiction for the best part of the last century. They stared at her silently with their huge black eyes and their grey, leathery skin. She stared at them, feeling woozy. For some reason, she didn't feel scared or amazed by them. She felt nothing towards them. Neutral. Not because they were kindly, but because they didn't look real. They didn't seem real.

This definitely wasn't right. These grey aliens were fictional. This wasn't like in her stories. They weren't real. She knew it instinctively.

"Welcome," the one grey alien said. "We are visitors from a far-distant region that neighbours the

Pleiades star system. Perhaps some of you have heard of it. We have come to initiate an exchange program."

Cate's head began to throb unbearably. Her vision began to blur and flash between two different images, between reality and this visual construct. For a moment, the room looked different and the abductees blinked out of view, reappearing just as quickly. After all, the aliens could cloak their ship; she was certain that they could also easily distort her perception.

Given the situation, Cate found a bravery that shocked her. She spoke up. "This is all lies! You are deceiving me! What is this nonsense?"

The abductees stared up at her in silent horror of her defiance. She winced, screaming out in pain as her brain tried to defy her. Her vision glitched, momentarily seeing beyond the illusory facade.

"Why not show your true faces? I know that this is a constructed hallucination. You are hiding your true faces and intentions behind a front that my brain can handle. This is a human's idea of a spaceship and aliens. This isn't the truth. I know it."

The so-called grey aliens glared at her. Cate realised they knew that she was aware something was amiss, more than the image they pertained.

One of the grey aliens came towards her. She realised that when it had been talking, its mouth hadn't even been moving. It had just stared at her with its huge, inky black eyes. This unnerved her.

She knows.... she heard one of them say, a male

voice, but it was a voice in the back of her head, rather than a sound that was captured by her ears. Hearing this felt unusual, like their true language was being masked by a layer of telepathic translation.

Should we show her our true selves? another one said, a female voice this time.

Yes, I think she can handle it. That's why we've been monitoring her. That's why we brought her up here. Perhaps we were wrong to use hallucinatory deception as our introduction... the male voice answered her.

She sat there listening to the voices that seemed to be inside her head, but also outside of it.

We had to. We couldn't just show her our true selves at the first instant. Her brain would go into meltdown.

Cate began to panic.

She is becoming hysterical. Calm her, the male voice instructed a smaller grey alien, who walked towards her.

The alien put his hands upon her shoulders. Cate felt instantly relaxed. Everything felt lighter now. Her blurry vision had gone and her consciousness felt free and light. She stared into its huge black eyes and felt a sense of serenity. She could sense it was a male. Even though it didn't have an apparent gender, it had a male-type of energy. Its skin had no lines or folds whatsoever. It felt cool to the touch. In a twisted way, she felt at one with the whole experience.

This is why the aliens have selected me, because I

am more aware than most humans. I have the appropriate brain mechanisms and perception to receive knowledge. I can handle whatever they want me for. They are gifting me with knowledge that most humans will never be blessed with, about what's really out there — esoteric knowledge about the universe and the true nature of things. I'm not suitable for alien-human hybrid breeding. Instead, they are using me as a conduit of knowledge. So it wasn't my imagination after all. I am a conduit. I knew it all along.

Cate felt horrified. Were any of her thoughts actually hers? Did she have any free will or was she an alien puppet that could be switched on and off, used at any moment, and without her ever even knowing? Made to instantly forget afterwards. She wrote her books thinking she was something special, that her imagination was special, but now she just felt like a fraud, like a puppet.

You are special. We don't control you. We are just using you as a conduit to get information out to the human race, the male voice said, inside of her head.

She wasn't sure she trusted them.

You can trust us.

"Can I?"

The hallucination was now fading and she was beginning to see the room properly. The room was constructed with otherworldly machinery that if she could explain it in physical terms didn't look wholly industrial but more biological. The fading abductees were sitting alone on the floor, staring up at nothing, still entranced by the aliens and their nonsense talk of unified galaxies. The humans must have been constructed figments of imagination, used to make her feel comfortable within this bizarre experience. She understood why they had done it, but it made her uneasy that they could manipulate her perceptions so easily.

The abductees faded, but her mum remained sitting in the middle. She was real. She was actually there.

"Mum!"

We didn't mean to bring her up with you. She'll be fine and won't remember any of this, the male voice said as instantly as she had begun to worry about her; the precise moment the feeling had turned into a thought. They must have been talking to her telepathically.

Cate was sure she believed them, that she'd be fine. She wondered if she'd remember any of this, too, rather than having a bizarre and unexplainable feeling that lingered over her; a feeling she often couldn't place.

If you choose to, but only if you can handle it. You've done better than last time, the male voice answered her thoughts.

Last time? Cate didn't remember last time, obviously because she hadn't been able to handle it. That being said, she wondered if this was all a hallucination too, a better constructed, more modern vision that would sit better with her beliefs about what she imagined aliens to be like, and the true aliens still hid behind this visage, while they were doing whatever they wanted to do to her mind, to her body.

She's a clever one to realise, the female voice responded to her thought. *Most never realise.*

"Stop playing with me!" Cate tried to shout, but she couldn't repel the grey alien's hypnotic, sedative effect.

Such big, black eyes...

And on that, she realised that it was another hallucination, but she felt so calmed by the hypnotic, fake grey alien that she didn't mind. She guessed he must be what she wanted to see: a 'friendly' alien. She was thankful for that.

Maybe I'll never be able to handle the true visage of the governing aliens that speak to me telepathically. But I want to see...

We could try, the male said in response to her thoughts.

But what if it doesn't work and I freak out and can't handle it?

Then you simply just won't remember, the male answered. *We will make you forget. There's no harm in trying.*

Cate tried to feel uneasy, but she physically couldn't rouse the emotion within her, as she was sedated by the touch of the grey alien.

Be careful though, the shock can send the brain

into trauma and then we'll be back at the beginning...
the female warned the male.

I think she can handle it.

I disagree. Her brain might be advanced, but I don't think she can handle it yet. I doubt that humans will ever be ready to handle it. I'm just concerned that's all, the female said.

I think she'll be fine, the male said. *Do you want to see?*

I do.

There was a flash of light and she saw the reptilian features of the governing aliens. Another hallucination? And then she saw beyond that, its fourth-dimensional face. A face that defied all logic. It was so bright and monstrous that she could barely focus or concentrate on it. It just didn't seem right that such a thing should exist. It disturbed her deeply, beyond any rational thought, a deep dread that made her bones ache. It had barely come into proper view when her brain decided it didn't want her to see. It prepared for the shock by shutting down. The bright lights were her brain not coping, like seeing a bright light and tunnel when having a near-death experience. Cate went into meltdown and started to have a seizure.

I told you to be careful, that this wouldn't work yet... she heard a distant female voice say. *Pull her out of it. Now we have to start our work all over again...* she sounded angry at the male energy who had fallen silent due to his misjudgement.

Cate hung onto this funny thought as she felt

herself blacking out, whilst the aliens put her into a sleep that would calm her brain and make her forget, that it seemed such a human trait for them to be squabbling. She was thankful that they were putting her out.

She could sense them moving around her, applying some sort of pressure onto her brain, without even cutting through her scalp. It felt tingly, like it was being massaged with a pulsating energy, as if it was calming the stress on her brain, relaxing the synapses so that the neurons didn't disperse the information that she was freaking out. She felt in a strange, heavy state of consciousness, like she was already asleep and dreaming, except she knew that she wasn't. There were flashes of vision around her as they got to work, murky shadows of figures beyond the shroud of fluctuating illusion, behind the comfort of ignorance.

She wasn't sure if what she was seeing was real or if the visions were internal because of the brain stimulation and rewiring. She was deeply fascinated by their advanced technology. The metallic spaceship she'd seen had also been an illusion, just like the physical appearance of the aliens. She realised that they weren't wholly physical beings, that they were able to travel through different states of matter in the same way that their spaceship could, using teleportation and accurate re-manifestation of matter through the interconnected quantum foam some humans call the aether. Even though they could easily create a machine capable of breakneck speeds, why travel along vast, never-ending regions of space when you could be a million light-years away in an instant?

She desperately wanted to know more about how it worked, how it was possible. These thoughts would come, in time. But her brain was currently struggling against it, deleting those thoughts from her mind, or perhaps moving them to be stored in another, more subconscious location; the thoughts that didn't readily form in her mind, betrayed by the gut instinct that plagued her that something was amiss during daily life. Or at least to pretend to herself that it was her imagination.

Many thoughts went through her mind in seconds while this happened. She felt like they had a connection, that they weren't going to harm her or her mother, especially with the concern in their telepathic voices. If the aliens had wanted to harm them, they would have, could have done it by now. After all, they could read her thoughts. She couldn't hide anything from them. Nor could she could protect herself from these all-seeing, mind-reading extra-terrestrial entities. She was obviously of some use to them, which is why they were so concerned with keeping her healthy, sane and alive. At least that's what she hoped. That's what she told herself.

The esoteric knowledge of the universe will come, in time, when I've been better prepared and can handle being a conduit, when I am ready. I am special. I am chosen. I look forward to receiving this information into my mind and be able to spread this knowledge through the guise of fiction stories. Who, after all, would believe it any other way?

Who... would... why... what...

She was suddenly struggling to form a coherent thought now.

What had I been thinking?

Everything she had considered within the last few moments now felt distant, murky, like grasping onto a stream of thoughts when delirious with sleep, and when wakefulness snatches them away.

Except rather than wakefulness, she felt like she was being snatched away by fatigue, falling deeper into a pleasant and calming slumber.

And with that, she was asleep.

* * *

The abductee lay on the table within the alien's constructed hallucination, awaiting the extra-terrestrial horror that was about to befall her. She knew that none of this was real, that this was an illusion of concrete reality created by a warped, deceptive extra-terrestrial perception.

Cate typed away like there was no tomorrow. She loved it when she was hit with a sudden burst of inspiration. Her science fiction stories always disturbed her. They felt so real, like she had actually experienced them. The details and the feelings she got when she imagined them were intense. She smirked to herself, glad that this was only fiction and not reality.

Gwen leaned over her shoulder to read what she was typing. She looked bemused. "I've no idea where you get your imagination from."

"Me neither. Like I said earlier, sometimes I wonder if it really is my imagination or if I'm channelling some sort of divine knowledge," Cate shrugged.

"I've no idea. Either way, it's wonderful. Fancy a break? We could sit outside with a cup of tea."

For some reason, an eerie feeling washed over Cate, and she suddenly felt uneasy at the thought.

"No, thanks. I'll stay inside."

She opened up a blank document on her computer. She'd thought of a new story idea.

She typed the title: The Conduit.

ODESSYA'S RAGE

"The museum is this way!" Yong-kook grabbed Seon-hwa by the arm, pointing down the road. Yong-kook had wanted to go to the park, seeing as it was a sunny day, but Seon-hwa had insisted a museum would offer more cultural value.

"No, it isn't! I know my way around Coventry. This isn't the way. This street just leads to more of those small, old-fashioned buildings and a chip shop," Seon-hwa said in annoyance, shrugging him off. The hot sun streamed down on him, making him prickle with sweat. He brushed his fingers through his dyed golden blond hair.

Yong-kook turned a map around in his hands, rotating it 180 degrees. He'd picked it up from the tourist office on the way.

"Are you sure?" he squinted, not being able to make out anything on the map.

"Yes, I'm sure! I've been a student here for nearly two years. I know my way around. I visit the local galleries regularly. We don't need a map. I know where we are," Seon-hwa said, lowering his sunglasses from his eyes.

"Okay. If you say so," Yong-kook shrugged, tossing the map into a nearby bin.

Seon-hwa closed his eyes and shook his head. Yong-kook never seemed to listen to him. He was always so distractible and impatient. Even though those qualities annoyed him, Yong-kook's aloofness was a welcome contrast to his own persistent seriousness.

"England is strange, but pretty. I'll have to come and visit you here more often, hyung," Yong-kook said. *Hyung* is an honorific term Korean males use to address male friends older than themselves.

"Please do," Seon-hwa smiled, resting his sunglasses atop his luxurious mane of blond hair.

They walked arm in arm down the shaded side of the street until they came to a large, looming, old-fashioned building. Its mixture of Victorian and Medieval architecture was striking and very beautiful. Gargoyles and grotesques sat watching on the jutting edges of the light brown stone, sitting neatly above the tall windows of the top floor. It was like a snapshot of a museum from a vintage postcard.

"Hmm, this museum was never here before," Seon-hwa said, staring up at the place. He narrowed his eyes and frowned. It gave him a deeply uneasy feeling. It didn't fit in with the rest of the buildings in the street. They weren't modern by any stretch of the imagination, but this place just seemed different.

"You sure you've been around this part of the town before?" Yong-kook asked in a relaxed fashion, seemingly unaffected by the weird sensations Seon-hwa was picking up from the place.

"Yes."

"You sure? You look confused."

"I told you I have been around here many times, nearly every day. This place was never here before. I'm sure there was a coffee shop here before and a pastry shop, not this... this massive museum," Seon-hwa swallowed, feeling anxious.

"You must be mistaken."

"I'm telling you, this place was never here before!" Seon-hwa raised his voice slightly.

"Well it must have been... Don't shout at me. You have such a temper these days," Yong-kook said quietly, lowering his gaze to the floor.

"I'm sorry, Yongi." Seon-hwa put his arm around him, staring into his deep dark eyes. Yong-kook always looked like a puppy when he was being scolded. Seon-hwa instantly felt guilty, so he hugged him.

Seeing their embrace, an old woman walking past gave them a funny look. Seon-hwa quickly pulled himself away.

"And now you deny our friendship because of a stranger's fleeting glance?" Yong-kook tutted. "I'm hurt. Some friend you are!"

"It's just that some westerners aren't used to seeing skinship," Seon-hwa explained. He felt his heart drop, and the smile dropped from his face, until Yong-kook started laughing.

"Oh, man. You are so serious lately, hyung!" Yong-kook punched him lightly on the arm.

Seon-hwa laughed, rubbing his arm. "Okay, you got me. I'll try to lighten up."

A few girls walked past them and smiled at Seon-hwa. He reciprocated with a coy smile, flashing his pearly white grin. He waved at them until they'd disappeared around the corner. They occasionally looked back at him and giggled.

"Who are they?" Yong-kook asked.

"They are students on my Curatorial Studies course at the university," Seon-hwa answered.

"Girls never admire me."

"I'm sure they do." Seon-hwa folded his arms.

"They don't. They always admire you instead. Can't say I blame them, though. You are incredibly handsome, so I just pale in comparison." Yong-kook stared at him in an admiring and affectionate way. Seon-hwa always dressed stylishly. Today he was wearing black jeans, black ankle boots, a dark grey shirt and ornate earrings. Seon-hwa studied art, but he always looked like a piece of art himself. "I wish I was as handsome as you."

Seon-hwa fanned his face with his hand, feeling hot and bothered. He felt surprised that Yong-kook considered him so good-looking. He wasn't sure what there was to be jealous of when Yong-kook was tall and handsome himself. "Thanks. But you're not so bad yourself. Maybe if you made an effort and combed your hair more often!" He ruffled Yong-kook's mane of short, thick, dark brown hair.

Yong-kook started to giggle, feeling embarrassed.

"Ah, get off. The wind messed my hair up! Are we going in this museum or not?" He pushed Seon-hwa off him.

"Sure. Seeing as I've never been in here before, let's check it out."

"I'm sure you'll be able to name all of the artworks, who painted what, and who sculpted what, and what year it was done, and which one-haired paintbrush was used — was it hair of horse or hair of camel?" Yong-kook babbled happily, jokingly. "You're so clever. You can educate me with your artistic and antiquities knowledge."

Seon-hwa smiled modestly. "Well, I should hope I can. I do want to be a curator one day."

They headed up the steps of the building, walking through two ridged columns that lined the entrance, and emerged into the foyer of the museum. They both stared around in awe, overwhelmed by its sheer beauty. Fantastic marble statues and magnificent paintings adorned the vast room. The floor was set in marble tiles and wonderful architectural stone pillars and podiums interspersed the artworks.

"This place is incredible. How have I never noticed it before?" Seon-hwa said breathlessly to Yong-kook as he headed over to a glass cabinet with a strange-looking bronze statue housed within it.

Yong-kook didn't answer. He'd walked off to another part of the room. His attention had been captured by a painting. He was never really that much into art like Seon-hwa was. He appreciated why people would like art, but he didn't really know all of the historical and technical details and abstract concepts like Seon-hwa did. But the painting was so beautiful that he was mesmerised by it. It was a painting of a merchant's port, somewhere wonderful like Venice.

For a moment, he could have sworn he saw the boats moving, could have sworn he could see the waves rippling and clouds rolling as if the painting was alive. He stared up at it in wonder, blinking rapidly. It was so beautiful. It was so unreal.

"Any leaflets explaining what the items are? There aren't any plaques on any of the artworks," Seon-hwa frowned. It was highly unusual. He'd never known it before in a gallery or museum. All items were usually aided by a descriptive plaque or at least decal lettering on the wall. But this time, there was nothing.

Yong-kook reached up to the painting to touch the moving boats.

"Yong-kook? Any leaflets?" Seon-hwa asked, looking around for him. He saw his friend staring up at a painting. "What's that?" he asked, heading over.

Yong-kook didn't answer.

Apart from their presence, Seon-hwa noticed that the place was empty. No staff, no other visitors. A sense of dread crept over him and he felt the hairs rising on the back of his neck. He wondered why he felt so uncomfortable in a setting he always felt so comfortable in.

"This museum looks lavishly expensive with this sumptuous decor and priceless artefacts. It's too fantastic to be overlooked by the general public. Why is the place so empty?" He frowned again, staring over at the open entrance door. Sunlight flooded into the room, highlighting the particles of dust floating within the air. A refreshing breeze cut through the stale air.

"I feel weird. Let's go, Yong-kook."

But Yong-kook was still reaching up to the painting. His fingertips brushed over the paintwork.

"Don't touch it!" Seon-hwa cried. "We'll get in trouble. You're not supposed to touch the artworks."

As soon as he touched it, the entrance door slammed shut. They both gasped, turning around.

"How did that huge wooden door slam shut? It was wedged open with a huge wooden doorstop," Yong-kook asked, wide-eyed, open-mouthed.

"I don't know. I'll try to open it," Seon-hwa said, darting off towards the door. He enclosed his hands around the doorknob and tried to turn it with all of his might, but it was no use. It just wouldn't budge.

Yong-kook quickly turned his attention back to the painting. There was no movement now. It was now completely still. He felt his heart sink, wondering if he'd imagined it. It was hot that day, but not hot enough to cause delirium.

"Any luck?" Yong-kook called out, keeping his eyes fixed on the painting.

"No. It won't open. I think we're trapped in

here." Seon-hwa rejoined him, trying not to panic.

Yong-kook was still entranced.

"I wanna get out of here. This place doesn't feel right. It feels spooky."

"I didn't have you down as a scaredy-cat," Yong-kook chuckled, glancing a look at him.

"I'm being serious. I had a bad vibe about this place before we even walked in. I should have trusted my instinct."

"Calm down. I think you're overreacting," Yong-kook said. "I'm sure we'll find another exit or a member of staff to open the door."

"What are you so mesmerised by?" Seon-hwa stared at the painting. Again, there was no plaque and he had no idea who had painted it. The style was unfamiliar. He felt increasingly frustrated.

"Nothing. Let's go this way." Yong-kook linked his arm through Seon-hwa's and pulled him away from the painting.

"Okay." Seon-hwa tried to calm down, but the anxiety that was rippling through him made him feel faint. He puffed his cheeks out, and walked with his friend through down a corridor and into a larger room.

They stared around in awe as they walked past fantastic statues carved from marble and stone. They stopped and gawped at a collection of statues set in rather erotic poses — half-naked men draped in cloth, long hair flowing behind them. All pure white in colour. Seon-hwa leaned in closer to peer at the detail — their facial features, the folds in the cloth, and the lines in their hair. The level of detail was so realistic that they looked like they could spring to life at any moment.

Yong-kook felt himself flush, and he looked away from the statues. Seon-hwa didn't appear to be bothered in the slightest by the statuesque nudity.

"Hellenistic style. They look so realistic. This level of detail is mind-blowing." He peered around for a plaque of some sort, but again, there was nothing. "I should know who carved something as amazing as this, but I don't." He furrowed his brow, feeling utterly perplexed.

"That's unlike you," Yong-kook said, still looking away.

"I've never seen anything in this museum before, not in books or on the internet. It's unusual."

Seon-hwa turned around to see Yong-kook's averted, sheepish gaze. "What's with you?" he pursed his lips, smiling knowingly.

"I'm just not used to it," Yong-kook blushed. "I don't wanna see half-naked statues, not with my friend anyway."

"You prude! They're only objects. Cold hard stone and marble. They're not real people." He knocked on one of them as if to illustrate his point.

"I know that," Yong-kook mumbled defensively.

"I love the feel of the cold, hard marble," Seon-hwa said, admiring a particularly beautiful statue of a young woman. She appeared to be the only female statue in the room. "I know I shouldn't touch, but…"

He bit his bottom lip suggestively, peering around. There was still no staff or other visitors around.

"You moaned at me for touching!" Yong-kook scowled.

"She's beautiful though, huh?"

"She's alright, I suppose, for a chunk of granite."

"Marble."

"Whatever."

"You don't see women this beautiful around here. I bet I could put some colour in her cheeks," Seon-hwa winked at Yong-kook.

Yong-kook didn't answer, staring blankly as Seon-hwa ran his hand down the smooth curve of the statue's back. As he ran his hand over the white statue, a peachy flesh colour began to appear. He blinked, frowning as he stared at it. He stared at the palm of his hand as if he'd somehow wiped away white paint, but there was nothing there.

"That's weird," Yong-kook said.

"Yeah…"

"If you think she's so beautiful, then why don't you kiss her?" Yong-kook glared, sounding offended, sounding almost jealous.

"Kiss a statue? What's gotten into you?" Seon-hwa raised his eyebrows.

"Yeah, seeing as you prefer cold, hard, lifeless objects to people."

"Wow, harsh."

"Bet you won't." Yong-kook folded his arms defiantly.

"Fine, but this is weird," Seon-hwa shrugged, placing a hand on the statue's arm to steady himself. He puckered his lips in a joking manner.

"You're weird."

Seon-hwa laughed at Yong-kook's remark, and then he kissed the statue on its cold, hard marble lips. The lips felt cold at first, but then they warmed up. He felt a bit delirious as he felt an unexpected sensation of passion flow through him. He'd only been joking about wanting to kiss the statue, but now he couldn't stop. He stared into deep blue, glowing eyes and felt entranced, powerless to resist. He felt an arm enclose around him, soft and tender, hands running through his hair. His sunglasses fell from his head and clattered to the floor. The touch felt so sensuous.

"Hyung..." He heard Yong-kook's voice. Somehow, it sounded distant, even though he was standing right next to him.

Seon-hwa kissed the statue passionately, feeling like he was getting lost in it. He began to unbutton his shirt. The statue's lips felt so full, soft, real and warm. He kissed them back, running his hand up the smooth, now warm flesh, and around the statue's neck into her soft flowing hair. He felt powerless to stop. He didn't want to stop this sudden passionate embrace.

"Seon-hwa!" he heard Yong-kook yell and he felt an arm pulling him backwards.

He disconnected himself from the statue and he gasped as a real, live woman stared back at him in place of the statue. She had the same features as the statue, but instead of the white marble, she was now in full blazing colour. Long flame-red hair fell down to her waist in luscious curls and the white cloth of her dress flowed behind her as if there was an invisible wind upon her. Her beautiful long white dress accentuated her stunning, slim figure. Her eyes twinkled green now instead of blue. They both stared at her in awe. She was a heavenly beauty. She looked far too beautiful to actually exist.

Seon-hwa fell to the floor in shock, Yong-kook catching him in his arms.

"Seon-hwa, the statue came to life!" Yong-kook squeaked, his voice trembling. She smiled coquettishly, her lips parted as she gazed at them in a shrewd manner that betrayed the innocent and youthful appearance of her face.

She reached her hand out to Yong-kook, her slender fingertips brushing his hand. He flinched, pulling his hand away from her.

She frowned at his response and took a huge, floating step towards him, dress billowing behind her. "You dare to deny my advances?"

"Wh-what?" Yong-kook stammered, bewildered by her forthright manner.

"Don't you think I'm beautiful?"

"I guess so..." he mumbled, looking startled.

"You only guess so? Are you saying that you do not find me attractive?" She looked affronted.

Yong-kook didn't answer her.

"There was a time when every man in the land

found me irresistible," she said bitterly.

Yong-kook frowned, taking an instant dislike to her, not keen on her neurotic and aggressive attitude. "I'm just still trying to process how a statue came to life."

"How are you real? Who are you?" Seon-hwa cut in, gripping tightly onto Yong-kook's arms.

"You awakened me from my slumber with your kiss. My name is Odessya."

"Is that Greek? Roman?" Seon-hwa asked.

Odessya smirked. "Clever young man. It's Greek. Young people have so many questions. What are your names? How old are you?"

"My name is Seon-hwa. I'm twenty-two," Seon-hwa answered suspiciously.

"I'm Yong-kook. I'm twenty."

"Ahh, so young and so beautiful. Pretty names, too. Perfect." Odessya took Seon-hwa's chin in her hand and turned his head from side to side, admiring his face as if he was a doll. "Porcelain complexion, luscious hair, beautiful eyes, youthful boyish but manly looks. I can tell you're intelligent and charming, too. You look like an angel. You're perfect."

Yong-kook also stared at Seon-hwa, mouth slightly open in awe.

He agreed.

Seon-hwa was perfect.

Odessya suddenly turned and smiled at Yong-kook as if she could read his thoughts. "You are very good-looking. You haven't quite blossomed yet, though. Give it time."

"Who are you to say who is beautiful enough to be perfect? Beauty is subjective. One man's trash is another man's treasure, and all that..." Yong-kook retorted.

Odessya just smiled, as if it wasn't worth the energy to debate with him.

"Get off me!" Seon-hwa struggled against Odessya's grip. Her fingers were pressed tightly into his skin. She felt unnaturally, inhumanly strong.

"And your body," she said calmly, letting go of his face. "I want to see it." She gazed down at his clothes. Her eyes glowed deep blue again.

Seon-hwa went into his trance-like mode again. He unbuttoned the rest of his shirt, took it off, and threw it to the floor. He then reached for the zip on his trousers.

"Hyung, what are you doing?" Yong-kook pulled at his shoulder, but Seon-hwa didn't respond.

"Oh my, nicely toned muscles. Such a young, well-proportioned body," she sighed, staring down at Seon-hwa's bare chest. She ran her hand down it.

"Get your hands off him!" Yong-kook shouted, his eyes alight with fury. She turned to face him, looking surprised.

"I've not collected a Korean from this time before. I like to collect Eastern Asians. They are very beautiful. You will make a great addition to my collection of beautiful men."

"Collection?" Yong-kook felt aghast as he stared around at the statues. "Were all these statues real men that you turned to stone?" He picked Seon-hwa's shirt up off the floor and scrunched it up into a messy ball of cloth.

"Yes," she replied simply, coldly. "This museum exists out of space and time. I can transport it to any time I want. I've collected the most beautiful men from each epoch, from the past, the future, from now... There is only now for me. There are so many beautiful men, but through the vibrations through the aether I can sense the ones I want to collect. I think it's a metaphysical pheromone attraction."

"How dare you! These people are not objects!" Yong-kook roared.

"They are now."

"Why would you do such a terrible thing?"

"I don't have to answer to you," she glowered.

"Seon-hwa!" Yong-kook yelled, shaking him by the shoulders.

No response.

"Seon-hwa, snap out of it!" Yong-kook hit him round the head.

Seon-hwa was whacked out of his reverie. "Ow!" he rubbed his head. "What's going on? Why am I half naked?" he gasped. His hands flew up to his chest in a protective manner.

"I was admiring your beauty, your youth and your perfection," Odessya said, floating barefoot along the floor towards him. She affectionately ran her fingers through his blond hair.

Seon-hwa was entranced by her glowing blue eyes. They were so mesmerising. He sighed. Her touch felt so pleasant and relaxing. It was as if she was emitting a magical pheromone that he felt powerless to resist.

"So what if I'm beautiful? It makes me fortunate, but it doesn't make me better than anyone else," he said dreamily.

"Only beautiful people are so dismissive of their beauty because they take it for granted. They don't know what it's like to hunger for beauty. They don't know what it feels like to be average or ugly, to not be wanted, only once they lose their beauty," Odessya sneered, suddenly gripping his shoulders tightly with both hands, staring contemptuously into his eyes.

"Beauty isn't everything. What about personality? What about intellect? What about intention? It's what's inside that counts," Seon-hwa winced. His head hurt. It physically hurt to disagree with her. "Why are you so shallow?"

"Shallow? My dear boy, I am the opposite of shallow. I've been alive for a long, long time. I've seen endless generations of people perish. Such beautiful people dead and gone. What is human life except for death waiting to happen?"

"That is a morbid way of looking at life," Seon-hwa frowned. He was confused as to why she seemed so wise and bitter when she only looked to be in her early twenties, far too young to be tainted by the concepts of which she spoke about in such a severe manner.

"I am realistic. You all take your beauty and your youth for granted. You think you'll look like this forever, but you won't."

"I think you've been reading too much Dorian Gray," Seon-hwa tried to shake himself free from her grip, feeling scared of her strength and her sudden anger. Her erratic mood scared him.

"Who?" Odessya asked.

"Never mind."

"You have a vague idea of death, but you don't know what it really means to be gone forever."

"You're right, but death would spare us of that torment."

"I am not so fortunate. A human lives for such a short time in the infinite span of time, in a certain specific time of which they know no other. A human is defined by the time and world they live in. But I am now. I am all times. Imagine if you were born in any other time, how many people you would have the chance to fall in love with, to be with. I am of a transient and never-ending nature that I can experience loves from different times, loves I would never get the chance to meet if I was constricted to a certain time, if I was a mere mortal." She loosened her grip on Seon-hwa's shoulders, realising she was hurting him, softened by her philosophical mood.

"A mere mortal?" Yong-kook repeated, eyes wide, suddenly realising what she was saying, but feeling too shocked to question it.

"You're crazy," Seon-hwa shook his head.

"I am a romantic," she seethed, glaring at him. She suddenly let go of him, walking up to a statue of a man. She placed her head on his shoulder and stared up at him longingly. She sighed sadly. "It saddens me that you both think of me as shallow and think I treat men like objects. That is not the case. It is because of my affections for them and a desire to preserve them in their most beautiful, glorious forms is why I turn them into statues. I am always heartbroken when someone dies, especially people I have affections for. I want to stop the heartache caused by illness, injury or death. Thanks to me, they remain young and beautiful. Forever." A tear rolled down her cheek.

Yong-kook pressed himself to Seon-hwa's back. They both stood frozen to the spot.

"But what if those men are not in love with you? Love isn't always reciprocated," Seon-hwa shook his head.

"I am aware. I only pursue men that are attracted to me in the first place. Attraction turns into love. I just speed up the process."

"With your blue eyes?" Yong-kook asked.

Odessya shot him a wry look, hateful and admiring in the same instance. "Who are you young men to question me?"

"That's wrong. You can't force people to love you," Seon-hwa scowled.

"Nobody has reign over me. I can do what I

want." Odessya's expression turned foul again, an aggression to cover her vulnerability.

She walked back over to Seon-hwa and rubbed his cheek tenderly with the palm of her hand. He flinched, thinking she was going to hurt him, but she then walked away. She walked a few steps to the left, her dress billowing behind her. She stopped at a painting framed in a thick gold frame. It didn't depict an image. It was dark, flat, painted a sludgy mixture of different shades of brown and black with hints of colour underneath. She held her palm out flat, inhaled deeply and blew across it. A white powder that resonated with a paranormal vibration blew across the air onto the canvas. The shimmering particles of glittery luminescence stuck to the wet paint.

They watched intently as each particle sank into the paint. They stared in disbelief as the paint started to bubble like tarmac melting under the hot sun. The whole image distorted until it settled back to its original flat brown sludge. She waited in silence, staring at the painting. An implacable, eerie oppressiveness cast itself over the room. The paint began to bubble, taking on a sticky bulbous form. It seeped over the edges of the golden frame, bubbling and becoming thicker, extending into a bigger form. Groaning sounds came from it, the shape of an arm appearing, a hand reaching out from within the bubble.

Seon-hwa and Yong-kook stared in horror at the mutating mass of paint as it took on a bodily form, its dark colour fizzing away and becoming lighter, becoming more flesh toned. Human characteristics began to appear, began to turn into someone they recognised.

The last remnants of the black paint fizzled away and a naked replica of Seon-hwa lay on the floor in a foetal position. His eyes shot open and he blinked rapidly. He took a sharp intake of air, sounding like someone coming up for air in the midst of drowning. With some effort, he managed to stand up. He stood there and stared at them blankly with large eyes.

Yong-kook's eyes went even wider as he stared at the naked replica of his best friend.

"What the hell?" Seon-hwa cried, staring at the naked version of himself. "How did you do that?" he roared at Odessya.

"I don't think you truly understood me, so I will show you what I meant. This is you now, but you'll age."

The replicant began to age dramatically, lines forming around his eyes, deep wrinkles lining his skin, his hair turning grey and his loose skin sagging over protruding ribs and hips. He looked like a bedraggled ninety-year-old man.

"You're just trying to scare me," Seon-hwa gasped at the sudden transformation.

"You'll decay."

The figure then began to cough blood, his skin turning jaundice and his milky eyes looking lost and empty.

"Stop this!" Seon-hwa cried, tears falling down his cheeks. He was shaking. "I don't want to see this."

Yong-kook gripped the shirt tightly in fright, but he too was unable to look away.

"You'll die."

The elderly version of Seon-hwa was hunched over. He started to cough and choke. His head fell backwards. A death rattle escaped from his throat, and the light went out in his eyes. The dead body floated motionless in the air.

"No!" Seon-hwa cried, aghast at what he was being forced to witness.

"You'll rot."

The corpse began to rot, his skin and hair receding, his skin decaying. Maggots ate away at him until there was nothing left but a horrifying skull and skeleton. It crashed to the floor. A pile of bones.

"And then beautiful Seon-hwa is no more. Gone forever," Odessya said calmly. Her lips curled into a sadistic smile.

Seon-hwa collapsed to the floor, sobbing. Yong-kook put his shaking arm around him.

"Don't you get it? *Carpe Diem*, my dear. Beauty is fleeting. Life is fleeting. That's why people attempt to hang onto it with all their might. Why do you think people have spent millennia carving images of beauty into stone or painting it upon canvasses or writing it into characters in novels? They want to immortalise beauty and the memory of life because it never lasts. But I can change that for you. I can spare you from these mortal processes. I can make you last forever."

"How?" Seon-hwa cried, staring up at her with wet eyes.

"I can immortalise you, like these people, forever cast in stone, forever capturing your youth and beauty. I can make you come alive whenever you want." She gripped the skirt of her dress and waved it over the body. When she pulled it away, the young naked figure of Seon-hwa returned. A young, fresh-faced beauty. He got up and walked towards them.

Seon-hwa rubbed his eyes, feeling raw with shock.

"Please don't listen to this twisted, cruel woman. She's off her head. Totally crazy!" Yong-kook seethed, but Seon-hwa was too traumatised to listen to reason.

"I'd be immortal, like you?"

"Yes."

"But I'd be trapped here?"

"Don't think of it as being trapped. Think of it as an escape." She took the skirt of her dress in her hand and waved it over the flat black painting. The image began to bubble again, colours appearing, forming a moving image; the animated painting of the Venice port Yong-kook had seen in the foyer. He hadn't imagined it after all.

"You can live in whatever beautiful reality you wish."

Seon-hwa scrunched his face up. "I can live in a painting?"

"Yes, in the art that so immerses you. I spent many years in bliss in my lover's arms, residing in the animated paintings of countryside or the beach ports. You can choose wherever you wish. It will seem real. Only your imagination can hold you back. Isn't that what you've always wanted — to escape from your dreary world?"

Seon-hwa nodded.

"Would it really be so bad to spend eternity with me?" she asked, eyes glowing a fierce luminous blue.

"You're so beautiful. It would be heaven," he smiled, hypnotised by her eyes.

"Stop this! Hyung, this woman is insane!" Yong-kook shook his head, feeling faint with anger and disbelief.

Odessya stepped up the conversation, her tone becoming more aggressive, blue eyes alight. "You'd never age. You'd never get ill. You'd never die. You'd be perfect for all eternity. Perfect as you are now. You wouldn't turn into a mere memory like everyone else."

"No, hyung. This isn't natural. She's just trying to scare you so she can add you to her collection."

Odessya burned with anger. Yong-kook was being too obstructive and it made her furious.

A crazed expression came over Seon-hwa's face. "No, she's right! Why would I want to get old and ill and die when I can live forever as I am now?"

Odessya smirked. "You are wise."

"No, you are being foolish, Seon-hwa! It's all

lies. Nothing can live forever. That's just the natural order of life," Yong-kook cried, pulling at his shoulders.

"Exactly! We've just witnessed the horror of the natural order of life in full graphic detail — illness, death, decay. But lucky for me I've met someone who can change that!" Seon-hwa shrugged him off and stood up.

"No!" Yong-kook was horrified.

"She knows more about life than I ever will. She's lived for centuries. She's an immortal being — proof that we don't have to grow old and die. What do I have to do?" he asked Odessya.

"Just take his hand." She pushed the replicant towards him.

Seon-hwa and his replicant faced each other, staring intently at one another.

"And then you can be immortalised."

"How do you know she's telling the truth? Why are you being so naive?" Yong-kook yelled.

"Because I have to believe in this!" Seon-hwa roared.

Yong-kook's eyes stung with tears.

"I love you, Yong-kook, but I have to do this."

Odessya's eyes suddenly flashed red with fury. She gritted her teeth and clenched her fists.

Yong-kook looked startled. "What?"

"You're my best friend. I have never loved anyone more in my life. You've always been there for me. I hope you can understand why I'm doing this. I don't want to be without you. Will you join me?"

Yong-kook looked at Odessya.

"You can be immortalised too, if you wish," she confirmed. "You can spend all eternity together in whatever heaven you choose." She looked straight into Yong-kook's eyes, blue eyes enticing him, daring him to accept the invitation to immortality.

He felt her blue gaze boring into his soul. He felt deeply uncomfortable. It felt like she could read his innermost thoughts and feelings. It unnerved him that his soul was laid bare to this neurotic, immortal predator.

For a moment, he considered her proposition.

"Yongi?" Seon-hwa asked weakly.

"No. This is wrong," Yong-kook finally conceded.

Odessya's lip twitched and she snarled, astounded that Yong-kook had disagreed with her. Nobody ever disagreed with her. Nobody ever had the willpower to fight her trance. She was even struggling with Seon-hwa due to Yong-kook's persuasiveness and their personal connection.

"Then I'm sorry," Seon-hwa snivelled, taking his replicant's hand. As their hands made contact, the double pulled him into an embrace. He began to turn into a luminous sparkling white powder that flowed over Seon-hwa. It rippled across him until it completely enveloped him. He then began to solidify into a white marble statue.

He finally set into a rigid, statue-like pose, a solid

stance staring blankly outwards.

"No..." Yong-kook slowly walked up to the statue of Seon-hwa. He stared at him, at his now even more flawless complexion, at the detail of his hair and muscles forever set into stone.

Odessya sneered, looking pleased with herself.

"And now you are beautiful for all eternity, cold and lifeless, just like you didn't want to be..." Yong-kook shook his head. "You fool, Seon-hwa!"

"He was a tough one to break."

Yong-kook felt mortified. He lay Seon-hwa's shirt over his shoulder and stared into his blank white eyes, not knowing what to do.

"You have both surprised me. Nobody has ever resisted my compulsion for that long. I had to appeal to his deep sense of mortality. I must be losing my touch. But he's mine now. My beautiful Seon-hwa," she giggled quite girlishly.

"You monster!" Yong-kook yelled at her, his eyes simmering with distress.

"Are you going to join him or not?" Odessya snapped.

"No," Yong-kook said defiantly.

"Then get out." She grabbed him by the throat and thrust him forwards. The sheer power of her grip made him fly through the doorway out into the museum corridor. He landed so roughly on the hard floor that for a moment he thought he'd broken his arm. A sharp pain shot up his spine. He groaned, rubbing his back. The door slammed shut behind him.

Yong-kook choked, his eyes watering. He rubbed his throat, wincing. His arm hurt, but it didn't feel broken. After a few minutes of recovering, and making sure his windpipe wasn't crushed, or that his back wasn't broken, he managed to right himself and get up. He pounded his fists on the door and tried to twist the doorknob open, but the door wouldn't budge.

"What am I going to do?" He walked listlessly down the corridor, back towards the foyer. The door was open again now, sunlight streaming in, inviting him to leave. He knew that if he left now, the museum would vanish and he would never get Seon-hwa back. He would be lost to him forever.

He closed his eyes. All he could see was the vision of solidified Seon-hwa. A vision that made his heart ache.

"No, I'm not going to leave you, Seon-hwa!" Yong-kook ran back into the corridor. There was a door open at the far end. He hadn't noticed it before. A flickering light was coming from inside, casting dancing shadows across the corridor wall.

Feeling apprehensive, he walked towards the room, peering into the open doorway. There was an old man sitting on a wooden stool. He wore rags, had a long, crooked nose, balding head and a long grey beard that fell down to his knees. Considering his grand age, he looked very strong, his arms bulging with worker's muscles. His back was arched over as he was busy making something on the table in front of him.

"Please, come in," the man said, without even turning around to face him.

Yong-kook cautiously walked in. The light from the flickering oil lamp lit up his face.

"Please shut the door behind you."

Yong-kook hesitated.

"There's no need to be scared of me. You've already faced the worst thing in this building."

"Odessya."

"Yes."

"What is she? She's not human."

"Far from it. She is an ancient Greek goddess."

"How is that possible?" Yong-kook raised his eyebrows in surprise. It sounded ludicrous, although it would explain the strange and impossible things he had witnessed.

"As I said, please shut the door, then I will tell you," the old man said calmly.

Yong-kook did as he was told, quietly closing the door behind him.

"Please sit down," the man said, pulling a stool up next to him. Its wooden legs dragged noisily across the concrete floor.

Yong-kook sat down gingerly. He peered around the dimly lit, relatively small room compared to the vast halls of the museum. This downtrodden shack of a room was a stark contrast to the grandeur of the rest of the building. The coldness of the damp brown walls made him shiver. A beautifully carved clay sculpture of a man in the corner of the room caught his attention. It looked like the statues they first saw in the gallery rooms. It had the same style.

"Please tell me more about Odessya."

The man pulled out two small cups and picked up an unlabelled bottle of alcohol. He pulled the cork out with a sharp pop then he poured out a measure into both. He drank his cupful and coughed.

"Odessya comes from a different culture and time to yours. She was spurned because her lover Alexander betrayed her. He loved and enjoyed every woman in the land except for her. She only ever cared for him, but he told her she was ugly and worthless. To get revenge on him, she took a lover of her own. Alexander found out. Even though he had countless lovers of his own, he was furious that Odessya would have the arrogance to betray him — a god. One day he got revenge on her and burned her alive."

Yong-kook gasped, putting his hand to his mouth. "How cruel. And she died?"

"No, she is an immortal goddess, so a mere fire wasn't enough to kill her. She remained alive, but as a withered husk. Her beauty was ruined. She was a burned shell of her former self. Alexander laughed at her and said, 'what man would want you now?' "

Yong-kook grimaced. "But she looked so beautiful when I saw her."

"She has god-like powers, so she maintains a false body — a false image."

"How could Alexander think she was ugly and worthless?"

"Alexander was a cruel and crazy bastard. He said she was ugly inside. People pray to gods like they are something divine, but they are just as messed up as the rest of us, if not worse. You must remember that these are gods from ancient times. They have an archaic mindset."

"I can't believe that gods and goddesses are actually real. Unbelievable." Yong-kook tried to fathom it all. "What happened to Alexander?"

"He moved on. I think that hurt her more than him being unfaithful and burning her alive, and ruining her looks, the fact that he just didn't care and just moved on like she was nothing to him."

"So that is why she collects the most beautiful men she can find? To get revenge on him and make him jealous in the hope he'd be sorry for what he did?"

"At first, yes, but her mind has become so warped over time that she's just gone insane. There was a time when she was sweet and kind. But of course, tragedy and bitterness can warp people. Alexander doesn't even care what she does or who she captures. That's if he's even still alive."

"Gods can die?"

"Of course. Everything dies eventually. Although I'm not sure how gods die. I've tried to kill Odessya many times, to no avail. I just don't have the power to end her," he gritted his teeth with fury. "Although I want nothing more."

"Then her promises of eternity were all lies."

"Of course they are. What she's doing goes against the natural order of life. She used to have empathy for the men she collected, but now she just turns them to stone and entrances them to cater to her every sordid whim. I think enough is enough."

"She captured my friend Seon-hwa," Yong-kook said glumly, staring desolately at his feet.

"I heard the commotion. I hear everything in here. I feel everything through the walls," the old man shuddered.

"I'm worried for him."

"Because you love him."

"As my friend."

"Yes, of course... I want to help you."

"Thank you. Who are you?" Yong-kook realised he hadn't even asked.

"My name is Myriod Cassellar. I was appointed as Odessya's personal sculptor. I was the best sculptor in the land. Oh, what an honour! Or so I naively thought. After being burned alive, she gave me the power to resculpt her face and body back to its former glory. We became good friends. I felt sorrow for her. I helped her during her most vulnerable moments. She initially asked me to sculpt men for her and bring them to life, but of course, they weren't real. They were just animated lumps of clay or stone. They soon withered and broke apart. She realised that you can't get better than a real-life person, with all their quirks, their flesh bodies, beating hearts, fears and desires."

"But they all died too?"

"Yes, she was horrified at the fleeting lives of mortal men and their fickle constitutions. It saddened her that she got to know them, fell in love with them, and then they died so quickly. She was always heartbroken."

So this was the story behind the beautiful monster. Yong-kook tried to stop himself feeling sorry for her. He couldn't allow himself to. Not after what she'd done to Seon-hwa.

"She instructed me to find a way to immortalise the men, so I fused my art with flesh and bone; the best of both worlds. I lengthened the lives of the men she found beautiful and worthy enough to be her lovers. She asked me to create this museum to house them all in, a metaphysical museum travelling through space and time collecting the most beautiful men from each epoch. Two thousand years later and we're still here, repeating the same toxic process for all eternity. This is heaven for her, but I am in hell."

"Why are you locked up in here if you are her sculptor, if you are her friend?"

"*Was* her friend. I'd already restored her beauty. She decided she didn't need me after that. She is the one with god-like powers after all, so she kept me captive in here. I can't leave the building. I've tried to escape many times. I believe she has forgotten about me."

"How can we stop her?"

"I've been formulating a plan. I've had more than enough time to think of every option available. I've turned my brains inside and out. But I think you are a blessing."

"How so?"

"Because you're not attracted to her. That rarely happens. She sensed that. She didn't like it. She can have anyone she wants, but you rejected her. Rejection is her biggest fear. It's thrown her senses off. We can use that to our advantage."

"Because she can't put me in a trance?"

"Exactly, my boy. She has no power over you, that's why she turned to violence and threw you out of the room."

"I wondered why her glowing blue eyes only seemed to affect Seon-hwa and not me."

Myriod pursed his lips, his expression lost in contemplation.

"So what's the plan?" Yong-kook asked impatiently.

"You see this statue I've been working on?"

"Yes." Yong-kook gaped at the tall statue of a man, nearly naked except for a cloth flowing around his waist. He had the finest features Yong-kook had ever seen — long, flowing hair, entrancing eyes — the finest form of a man with sinewy arms and a perfect torso and legs.

"Breathtaking, no?"

Yong-kook gulped hard and nodded. "I think if he was real, he would be the most handsome man I've ever seen."

No, the second most handsome, he corrected

himself, thinking of Seon-hwa.

"You're looking at the form of Alexander."

Yong-kook's mouth fell open. "No wonder Odessya was heartbroken. Who could ever match up to a man like that?"

"Alexander is the finest form of a man, but he had a cruel heart, there's no mistake." Myriod shook his head.

"So you want to bring Alexander back to life?"

"Only an animated statue of him to distract her long enough for us to get revenge on her. Her reign of lustful terror must come to an end."

"How are we going to stop her?"

"We're going to rescue your friend then we're going to burn this damn place down."

Yong-kook nodded, smiling smugly at the plan. He took the cup of alcohol and downed it in one. "I'm ready."

"Then we shall begin." Myriod opened a drawer underneath the table. He took out a folded piece of cloth. He opened it out to reveal a long brown lock of hair.

"This is Alexander's hair," he said, taking it in his hands. He held the end with his left hand, then enclosed his right hand around it and pulled it through.

"This plan can't fail. She will kill you otherwise and your friend will be lost to her forever."

"We won't fail." Yong-kook was sure he sounded certain, even if he didn't feel it. He had no other choice but to be hopeful.

"Then we shall proceed." Myriod walked over to the clay statue. He held his right hand out and blew across it. The same white powdery substance that Odessya had used to animate the replicant Seon-hwa rippled across the statue of Alexander. The particles settled over him, coating him in an iridescent white glow. The statue turned from sparkling white to full colour. He suddenly moved, coming to life, looking shocked as he took his first breath, but then immediately settled. He stood up and stretched his arms out. He looked so realistic, as if he was actually made from flesh and bone. The cloth fell down from his waist.

Yong-kook gawped at him as he stretched his arms over his head. He bent over and picked up the cloth, tying it around his waist to protect his modesty. He glowered, staring out into the distance, as if looking through the walls to where Odessya was no doubt cavorting with her captives.

"The replicant is ready."

"He looks so real. He's so beautiful. Can I touch him?" Yong-kook reached a hand out towards Alexander.

"No!" Myriod slapped his hand away. "He's just a replicant. He doesn't have the towering grandeur, or the burning cynicism, or the egotistical aggression that Alexander had. He was fearsome. Think yourself lucky that this is just a passive, animated shell. Let's go and distract her. I have the fire ready." He grabbed the bottle of alcohol and jammed it under his belt.

"Where?" Yong-kook looked around. The only fire he could see was the flickering oil lamp reflecting distorted shadows on the dark walls. He doubted that that would cause any substantial damage.

"Don't doubt me, boy. Just be prepared to save your friend when I light this place up. Be prepared to escape. That's all I want you to do."

Yong-kook nodded, not feeling prepared in the slightest, but Myriod and replicant Alexander were already walking out of the door. He hurriedly got up and followed them down the corridor towards the locked room.

There was a giggling from the other side of the locked door.

They stood in front of the door. Myriod broke a small piece of clay off Alexander's throat and swallowed it whole.

Yong-kook grimaced, wondering what on earth the old man was doing.

Myriod gagged as the lump of clay got stuck in his throat. He looked like he was going to choke, but then he settled down. He rubbed his thumb over Alexander's throat, rounding off the Adam's apple to look as it did before.

"Odessya! Open the door now!" Myriod mouthed, but Alexander bellowed the words as he stood staunchly at the doorway. Myriod was speaking through Alexander to give the illusion he was alive.

Yong-kook realised Seon-hwa's replicant had

never spoken a word because he too was just an empty shell of animated flesh.

The door creaked open. Odessya was cuddling up to a handsome captive. Her glowing blue eyes went wide with astonishment and her jaw fell open.

"Alexander?"

Yong-kook saw Seon-hwa's statue to the side of her. How long would it be before Odessya decided to play with him? A week? Six months? Ten years? A hundred and fifty years? She'd inflicted so much pain on the both of them and she'd already neglected him. Seon-hwa had given up his mortality in his emotional distress and he was already a forgotten plaything.

It made Yong-kook's blood boil.

Odessya would soon pay for this.

Alexander strutted into the room. With a strong hand, he grabbed the captive by the throat and threw him down to the floor. With fiery hazel eyes, he then glowered at Odessya.

"Alexander, is it really you?" Her voice quivered.

"Yes."

Odessya gasped and started to cry. Her eyes settled back to green. "Why did I not sense you?" She ran her hands over his face, staring longingly into his alluring eyes.

"It has been a long time since we saw each other," he shrugged.

She got closer to him. "Oh, Alexander. You're the most perfect man I've ever seen. I've traversed the far reaches of time and mankind, and as hard as I have tried, I have never found anyone as perfect as you. You were always the one for me." She stroked his face tenderly, crying as she kissed him on the lips. "I've never loved nor hated anyone as much as you. So why do I feel nothing right now?"

Alexander remained silent, stoic.

"You'll pay for what you did to me!" she roared, her expression full of fury as she thrust her hand into his chest.

Alexander didn't scream. He didn't cry. He didn't move an inch. Odessya pulled her hand out of his chest. Instead of his heart in her hands, she had a huge lump of clay in her grip. Her eyes went wide in realisation.

"A replicant!" she snarled, throwing the clay to the floor. "That's why I didn't feel anything."

"Yes," Myriod said, walking into the room.

"You!"

"A damn perfect replicant to fool you, even for a moment. I was the best sculptor in all of ancient Greece after all."

"You'll pay for this!" she cried, knocking Alexander's head off his shoulders. It fell to the floor and splattered on the ground like a pumpkin.

"No. You will pay for what you have done to all of these innocent, impressionable men, and to me. I left my family to be your servant, and yet you discarded me just like all your other playthings."

"You treacherous bastard!" Odessya shrieked, her hair flying up around her, her eyes radiating blue.

Myriod took the bottle of alcohol from his pocket, took a deep mouthful then swirled a finger around in his mouth. All of a sudden, he blew out a stream of fire right onto Odessya.

Her blood-curdling screams rang out as the fire enveloped her body. She clawed at her face, reliving the pain she'd gone through whilst being burnt alive. She fell backwards, a flaming mass, and landed on the sofa she'd been canoodling on. It also went up in flames. The smell of burning flesh and the sounds of agonising screams froze Yong-kook to the spot.

"Get your friend and get out of here!" Myriod roared at him.

Yong-kook snapped himself out of his shock and ran past Odessya, the flames licking at his side.

"Seon-hwa! Snap out of it." He put his hands on the shoulders of the statue.

Somehow, Odessya had managed to put herself out. Yong-kook gasped as he saw the burnt husk of a woman hulking towards him. His face contorted in terror and he reeled backwards in an effort to get away from her. Upon seeing his disgusted expression, she started to cry out in misery and pain.

"How could you do this to me, Myriod?" she cried, her voice weak from agony. "How could you make me relive my deepest, darkest agonies?"

"Because I want to escape this hell. I want you to die!" Myriod shouted, reaching for his bottle.

"Seon-hwa! Please turn back to normal. You thought you were immortalising yourself because you were so afraid of death and decay, but then you sacrificed your life. You sacrificed your freedom for false promises. You're still not living while you're trapped in this beautiful shell. Life is so precious because it is fleeting, that's what makes it so beautiful and that it's unique to us. Knowing life will end is the only thing that makes life worth living!"

Odessya managed to laugh. A bitter, twisted laugh that caught Yong-kook off guard. "Oh, you're suddenly quite the philosopher now, aren't you, boy? You talk about emotions like you're being honest about yours," she bellowed with real vitriol in her voice.

"What do you mean?"

"The fact that you can't even admit you're in love with Seon-hwa! You foolish boy. I know you love him. That's just one reason why you weren't attracted to me," she cried from the orange flames that engulfed her, staggering across the floor towards Myriod.

Yong-kook closed his eyes, tears trapped beneath his eyelids. He felt himself trembling with sadness and anger.

How dare she.

After everything she'd done — assaulting them both, traumatising them with disturbing art magic and imprisoning Seon-hwa in a statue — after all that, how dare she be so inconsiderate as to force him to reveal his secret feelings for Seon-hwa as if it was nothing. Of course it was nothing to her, but he always wanted it to be his decision when to be honest about his feelings, not anyone else's. Any sympathy he felt for her while listening to her tragic past had now vanished.

There was a gurgling noise as Odessya reached out a blackened hand towards Myriod, grasping his throat tightly. Myriod managed to push her off, setting forth another burning stream of fire around the room. The frozen captives began to burn.

"Noooo!" she screamed. "My beautiful statues!"

Yong-kook shook himself from his thoughts. He suddenly panicked, feeling the flames lapping around them. He attempted to pick up the solidified Seon-hwa, but he was far too heavy and wouldn't budge.

Yong-kook felt defeated. The fury he felt for Odessya suddenly and unexpectedly diminished. Perhaps she was right. Perhaps he should have been more courageous about his feelings sooner. But like her, he too was scared of rejection. He wondered that if it was so obvious to her, had it always been obvious to Seon-hwa?

"God damn it," Yong-kook gritted his teeth, tired of his thoughts going around in circles. He took a deep breath. "I love you, Seon-hwa."

Seon-hwa's blank white eyes stared back at him.

"I might as well tell you honestly how I feel now we're going to die. I was always scared of how you'd react if I revealed my true feelings for you, but I love you. I think you're perfect." He closed his eyes and kissed him on his cold marble lips.

Yong-kook's face was wet with tears. Through

physical contact, the natural pheromone attraction awoke the statues from their slumber. But Seon-hwa remained cold and solid.

Yong-kook felt faint. He thought the flames were burning his lips up along with the rest of him, and for a moment, in his turmoil, he didn't care if the flames took him away, but he suddenly felt the cold lips becoming warmer. Seon-hwa put an arm around him, reaching his hands up into Yong-kook's hair and tenderly kissed him back.

"Seon-hwa!" Yong-kook cried, tears falling down his cheeks.

He had returned to him.

Seon-Hwa tenderly placed a hand upon the side of Yong-kook's neck. He smiled modestly and gave him an understanding look that said a hundred things at once. He turned to see the statues all melting, burning, all dying. Odessya's promise was a stretched truth, a lie. Lengthened mortality was not immortality.

"I was a fool. Thank you for saving me. The fire... Let's get out of here," he said, grimacing at the intense heat of the flames. He grabbed Yong-kook's hand and they bolted towards the door.

Yong-kook noticed the shirt draped over Seon-hwa's shoulders was falling down. He snatched it off him and gripped it tightly as they ran.

Myriod was overcome with flames.

"Myriod! Let me save you," Yong-kook reached down to him, coughing from the smoke fumes, eyes watering so much he could barely see.

"No. You must go. I want to die so I can finally be reunited with my family. I believe in the natural order of things, not this mockery of immortality. My spirit will live on properly, as it was supposed to two thousand years ago."

Yong-kook didn't know what to say.

"I told you to get out of here!" Myriod waved his arm in the air. Odessya was climbing onto him, a demented, burnt figure, eyes lit with sheer fury. They looked away as Odessya thrust her hand into his chest.

"Thank you. I can finally be at peace," he croaked.

They heard a horrific squelching noise as Odessya killed Myriod. The light went out in his eyes, his head fell to one side, and he became motionless.

Horrified and speechless, Seon-hwa and Yong-kook ran through the doorway. Odessya ran after them, snarling and screaming. The building vibrated around them, parts of the roof falling down, the fire spreading.

"The door is open!" Seon-hwa shouted, pointing at the stream of light flooding in from outside. A huge chunk of ceiling narrowly missed them, cascading to the floor inches beside them.

"You can't leave! Don't leave me here alone!" Odessya screeched, but they ran through the doorway. A blinding white light enveloped their vision as they raced down the steps and down onto the street.

There was an almighty explosion from the building, sending out a shock wave. Seon-hwa grabbed Yong-kook and they both fell down to the hard ground. They covered their heads as debris cascaded outwards.

Unearthly screams hurt their ears.

They craned their necks around and peered up at the burning museum. Odessya's screams rang out as she burned in the doorway.

It was a terrible sight. A mixture of emotions hit them. Yong-kook put a hand over his mouth and Seon-hwa looked away.

It appeared that she couldn't leave the building. She was trapped, unable to die, forever looking like her worst nightmare, forever trapped in the prison of her own making. The building became faint, glitching as it disappeared to another time. The sounds of anguished screaming stopped. The original building Seon-hwa walked past every day suddenly reappeared in its place. The museum had vanished. The air felt lighter now, less oppressive. The debris had also vanished from the phantom incident.

Yong-kook helped Seon-hwa to his feet. They stared at each other for a moment, trembling in silent horror, then fell into each other's arms and hugged each other tightly. The old woman from earlier walked past again, staring at them quizzically.

Yong-kook quickly grabbed the shirt off the floor and placed it around Seon-hwa's bare shoulders to protect his modesty from the old woman's prying eyes.

Despite feeling traumatised, bewildered, battered

and bruised, Seon-hwa managed to laugh.

"Hyung?"

"Yes, Yongi?"

"Next time let's just go to the park."

* * *

A year later, Seon-hwa was standing on a stage about to give a speech to his university class.

The students and press all filtered in and found their seats. Yong-kook found his seat and sat there quietly watching Seon-hwa. He stood confidently on the stage, adjusting his microphone.

"Good afternoon, everyone. Thank you for gathering here today. My name is Choi Seon-hwa and I'm the leading curator of Ancient Greek discoveries at the National Museum — specialising in classic sculpture and antiquities."

The press all talked over each other in an effort to get him to answer their questions.

"Mr. Choi, it's unusual and impressive for a student to become a high-profile curator before they've even graduated university. And at such a young age. You're only twenty-three?" a reporter asked.

"That's correct."

"What led you to the discovery in Greece five months ago?"

"At the time I was reading a lot about Greek mythology, about a lesser known goddess called

Odessya and her tragic love story with her lover, Alexander," Seon-hwa bent the truth. He could hardly say he spent time with an ancient Greek goddess in a metaphysical museum that defied the natural laws of physics and moved outside of time and space, and also that he discovered metaphysical sculptures that defied natural laws of biology and matter, becoming one of those sculptures himself! They would think him crazy.

"It was said that Odessya appointed the best sculptor in the land as her personal sculptor, a man named Myriod Cassellar. It was said that he created sculptures as amazing as all of the greatest classic sculptors — like Bernini and Michelangelo — incredibly detailed sculptures that looked like they could come to life at any moment, which sounds amazing on paper, but then I thought *what if this man actually existed? What if this myth was based on a real-life sculptor?* It was a long shot and a crazy idea, but I began to research into the censuses of people from that time period. I didn't think I was going to find anything, but I found traces of information about a man named Myriod Cassellar who lived in 200 B.C. Greece, just before the empire fell. I then joined an archaeological team in the area. I tipped them off about my information and the possibility. They humoured me and let me accompany them on a dig in the area I thought Cassellar lived in. We were astonished to unearth a massive amount of undiscovered sculptures in the area, figures in exquisite detailed marble, stone and clay. Just as the myth had described."

Yong-kook smiled wistfully, thinking about his fiercely brave friend Myriod.

"The discovery is said to be one of the biggest finds of this century," the reporter said.

"Yes, I've had the discovery documented by the international media and chronicled in the best archaeological magazines. I'm very pleased."

"What do you aim to do now?"

"I hope to graduate university. I have been writing my dissertation on Myriod Cassellar: the undiscovered great."

"I'm sure there will be no doubt of your graduation with first class honours. Would you like to open your own museum?" a different reporter asked.

Seon-hwa cringed as he thought about the experiences he'd had whilst in the metaphysical museum, but he knew that was a one-off occurrence. He hoped. At least he'd been fortunate to turn the situation to his advantage; he'd made a burgeoning career and fortune from that bizarre experience. "It's a possibility. Thank you for all your questions."

"Wait. I have a question!" a woman threw her hand up in the air.

"Me too!" a professor called out.

Yong-kook watched as the reporters, academics, students, and general members of the public all clamoured to ask Seon-hwa questions, dozens of voices all talking at the same time, dozens of eyes upon him. He felt so proud of him.

Seon-hwa looked over at Yong-kook and smiled bashfully, his eyes turning into pretty half-moons.

Yong-kook smiled back.

He was perfect.

ABOUT THE AUTHOR

Natalie Rix lives in the West Midlands, England. She loves to write stories which are a mixture of horror, sci-fi, and anything weird or wonderful. She also writes children's books under the pseudonym Madeline Pope. She published her first book "Rodney and Splodge go to Topaz Town" in 2014. It was well received by local children and adults alike. She hopes to continue to publish more work through her publishing company, Monnath Books.

For more information please visit:
www.natalierix.com and www.monnathbooks.co.uk

Acknowledgements / References

Front matter quote:

https://en.m.wikipedia.org/wiki/Aether_(classical_ele
ment)

https://en.wikipedia.org/wiki/Akasha

Edgar Cayce, American Mystic - 1877 – 1945. Page 40.

Quote by Lucius Annaeus Seneca, (or Seneca the Younger), Roman Philosopher, Statesman and Dramatist - 4BC – 65 AD. Page 88 and page 90.

Niels Bohr, Danish Physicist - 1885 – 1962. Page 119.

Michael Talbot, American Author - 1953 – 1992, **The Holographic Universe**, 1992. Page 123.

Oscar Wilde, Irish Author, Poet and Playwright - 1854 – 1900. **The Picture of Dorian Gray**, 1890. Page 220.

Bernini, Italian Sculptor and Architect - 1598 – 1680. Page 249.

Michelangelo di Lodovico Buonarroti Simoni, Italian Sculptor, Painter, Architect and Poet - 1475 – 1564. Page 249.

Made in the USA
Columbia, SC
04 February 2018